For Terry
My writing best friend
Who believes, even when I don't

Part One

Chapter One
1977
Dimension AG54298-M85677

F*inally, I can kill myself.*

Michael Hollister pushed his face against the bars of his cell. He was alone for a moment, a brief reprieve in what had become his personal hell. Beatings. Rape in its many varieties. An endless cycle of horror and ignominy. He wasn't strong enough to fight off even a single hardened thug, much less a pack of them. The inmates of C Block found such a fresh young prisoner an unusual treat.

Michael removed the sheet from his bed and twisted it. *If I mess this up, they'll put me on suicide watch. That'll make this just that much harder.*

Now that the moment had arrived, with the jury-rigged noose actually in his hands, he didn't stop to consider whether he really wanted to end his life. It was all he had thought about since he'd arrived in the Oregon State Penitentiary.

There is no Hell an angry God can create that will be any worse than this life.

Happy thoughts of ending it all and escaping the humiliation and pain had allowed him to survive with his mind intact. Now was his chance. He twisted the other end of the sheet tight and fixed it around the top post of the bunk. He had to make do—and to make haste.

He tied the other end around his throat, paused for just a moment, remembered the feeling of his hands around Carrie Copeland's neck, and smiled for the last time. He jumped slightly and let himself fall, a dead weight. He hoped to break his neck.

He did not. The sheet tightened and choked him. Michael's eyes bulged, his face turned first red, then a deep purple. His bare feet beat an involuntary staccato tattoo against the concrete floor. His arms never left his sides. His last thought before consciousness deserted him was, "Will this never end?"

Eventually it did.

Chapter Two
1966
Dimension AG54298-M85678

Michael Hollister opened his eyes.

The room was dark and cast mostly in shadow, but he recognized it even so—his childhood bedroom. He held his hand in front of his face. His long, thin fingers were gone, replaced by short, chubby ones. He touched his neck. No sign of strangulation. He tried to get out of bed, but fell face-first to the floor. It was much farther down than he had anticipated. His bed seemed enormous.

He crept down the hall to the bathroom, closing the door behind him. He flicked on the light and blinked back the brightness. When his vision cleared, he gazed into the bathroom mirror.

Michael looked into his own childish face.

What. The. Fuck?

Michael's hand went to his cheeks. Chubby. Soft. He flexed his fingers. Short. Weak.

His legs went weak and he sat down with a thump on the toilet seat.

Holy shit. How the hell did this happen? He got to his feet and looked, fascinated, in the mirror. He raised his eyebrows, watching his boyish image do the same. He closed his eyes, shook his head violently from side to side. When he opened them, it was all unchanged.

He opened the bathroom door and walked, automatically, through the house and back to his bedroom. His family had lived in the same house since he was born, so, aside from a few cosmetic changes, this house was the same as the one he had been living in until his arrest for murder, just before his high school graduation.

He climbed back onto the bed.

I killed myself. That should have been the end of it. Instead, I woke up here. So. There is something other than devils with pitchforks or the long dirt nap on the other side. Interesting. And now, here I am, in the body of a child. It's a clean start. No prison, no murder. I can do anything I want.

Outside, a breeze kicked up. The house creaked. Michael froze, eyes on the dim slit of light at the bottom of his door. His heart pounded.

If he comes in here ... what? If he comes in here, what will I do? Bunch up my little muscles and scare him away? He would like that.

Again, Michael slipped out of bed and crept through the house. He went downstairs to the kitchen and pulled a carving knife with a bone handle out of the block on the counter.

Back in bed, he slipped it under his pillow.

Better.

Michael lay back against his pillow, thinking furiously.

Eventually, dim gray light began to show around the edges of his curtains. Michael sat bolt upright.

Time to get some answers.

He pulled the knife from beneath the pillow and got out of bed, less awkwardly this time.

Already getting used to this shitty little body.

He walked silently down the thick carpet runner that ran the length of the hall. He opened the door to his parents' room and peered into the semi-darkness. Two forms in the bed—his parents, Clayton and Margaret Hollister. Michael's lips pulled back in disgust.

Finally.

"Father," Michael whispered. A child's voice.

His father blinked once, twice, then focused on Michael.

He's younger, too. Of course.

"What the hell? Michael, what are you doing? Get back to bed."

In one smooth motion, Michael pulled the knife from behind his back and jammed it into his father's throat.

Blood spurted against the hand-tufted chenille bedspread and spattered onto his father's blue and gray striped pajama tops.

Michael pulled the knife back, giving it as much of a twist on the way out as he could muster. The handle was slippery with blood, and his hands were not strong.

Clayton Hollister's hands flew to his throat, but trying to stanch the blood flow was like trying to hold back the tide.

Margaret Hollister awoke, groggily lifted her sleep mask, and saw an Alfred Hitchcock movie come to life in her own bedroom. She screamed, loud, shrill, and long.

"Oh, *now* you have something to say, Mother? Where were you when I needed you?" His words went unheard in the reverberating screams that filled the room.

Michael stepped back and admired the tableau playing out before him. Clayton Hollister tried to speak, could not. Margaret Hollister tried to stop screaming, could not. Michael Hollister made no effort to hide his smile, which revealed two missing front teeth.

The Hollister bedroom, decorated in muted golds and taupe, was now splashed by crimson, arcing across the bed, the table, the floor. Clayton, gurgling, finally slumped back against the headboard, his eyes unfocused. His hands fell limply into his lap.

Michael nodded, satisfied. He wiped the bloody handle of the knife on his own pajamas. He closed his parents' door, muffling his mother's screams.

That was fun. But, now what? They would never convict a small child of murder, but there will be long years of doctors, therapy, drugs, treatment, people probing me. I don't think I can handle that. Still, the end is not the end. There is something after life. What if I kill myself again? Will I come back here? Somewhere else in my life? I'd rather not be a small child like this, if I don't have to be. There's only one way to find out.

He tossed the knife onto his bed and clambered up after it. He looked around at his childhood room. A picture of Winnie the Pooh and Piglet hung above his dresser. A toy box with a firetruck and a Slinky poking out of the top sat in one corner. His bed, dresser, and night table were a matched set.

Not a bad room. Would have been a good life, I suppose, if not for him.

Michael buttressed the knife against the mattress, pointed at his chest at a 45-degree angle. Before he had a chance to reconsider and change his mind, he drove himself forward onto the tip of the knife.

Michael Hollister screamed, but only for a moment.

Chapter Three
The Universal Center of Life

Darkness.
 Darkness.
Darkness.

Carrie Copeland opened her eyes. She gasped, and her hand flew involuntarily to her throat. After the peace, the quiet embrace of the darkness, the nothingness, the room around her was large, bright, and empty.

Wait. This isn't right. Where am I? I always wake up in the same place. I'm supposed to be on Mom and Dad's couch, with a stiff neck and the sun in my face.

"Hello." A honey-smooth female voice. A voice meant to soothe.

Carrie looked around. White walls, floor, ceiling. Rows of white benches that blended into the unrelenting whiteness. Aside from Carrie and the benches, the room was empty.

"Hello?"

"Welcome. I am Bertellia."

"I'm sorry. Who?"

"Bertellia. Your trainer, if you wish it."

Carrie touched a hand to her forehead. Closed her eyes for a beat, then two. When she opened them, everything was unchanged.

"Trainer?"

"Well, *guide* could work just as well. Or, *supervisor.* Whatever works. We don't get hung up on titles here. People who feel powerless need titles. We just are."

"I can't see you, and it sounds like you are sitting right next to me. Are you ... invisible?"

A laugh like wind chimes sounded from all corners of the room. "No, I am visible, and at the moment, made up of organic material, just as you are. I am simply elsewhere at the moment. Here, let me come to you."

Carrie jumped. A woman of indeterminate age sat next to her, where no one had been a moment before. She had long gray hair, pinned up. Her face was mostly unlined, but there were laugh lines around her eyes. She was dressed in long, soft robes the color of pale moonlight reflected on snow.

"Better?"

Carrie scooted away from her, eyes wide.

"Where am I? I know I died. I've done that often enough. But I always wake up in the same place, the same time—twelve years old, on my parents' couch."

"You were stuck, returning to the same spot over and over. Now, you are free."

"Stuck?"

Bertellia nodded gently. "You took your own life, which makes for an incomplete cycle, so you were started over. Each time you took your own life, you were started over. Your most recent life, you followed it to its conclusion."

"All those lives—why did I wake up in the same place and time?"

"This is eternity, but I still don't have time for all the questions you will want to ask."

"How about just that one, then?"

"Very well."

Bertellia smoothed a nonexistent wrinkle from her robe, which shimmered at her touch.

"You awoke at the same place and time because an algorithm in the Machine decided that was the place, the time, when things had gone awry for you. Or, the place and time where the Machine thought you had enough time to get your feet on the right path. I am not a cosmic mathematician, so I cannot fully explain it."

"Wait. The Machine?"

Bertellia raised her eyebrows. "One question, remember?"

Chapter Four
Dimension AG54298-M85679

Michael opened his eyes. He was back in his same childhood bedroom, darkened once again. The knife was gone. There was no pain.

He climbed down, padded silently down the hall and into his parents' room.

Inside, his father snored softly.

He's alive. Everything has been reset, exactly the same.

Michael went to the kitchen and retrieved the bone-handled knife from the block.

He walked up the stairs to his parents' room.

Chapter Five
Dimension AG54298-M85765

Michael Hollister killed his father eighty-seven more times. The scene played out the same each time, with minor variations. The knife, slicing his father's throat, then killing himself. Wash. Rinse. Repeat.

The well of anger and hatred inside him was deep.

The eighty-ninth time Michael opened his eyes in his darkened bedroom, he went downstairs, got the same knife, and returned to his parents' door. He stepped inside and watched them sleep, as he had so many times before.

He looked at the knife in his hand. Moonlight entering the window glinted softly off the blade.

I think I've killed him enough.

Michael returned to his room, slipped the knife under his pillow, and drifted off into a dreamless sleep.

Chapter Six

Carrie swept her hair from her eyes. It was the same haircut she'd had on her last day on Earth, when Michael Hollister had trapped her in the church and murdered her.

"Fine. So, I'm here, even though I have no idea where 'here' is. What's next, then? Judgement? Heaven, hell, or purgatory?"

"Ah. Of course, I should have realized." Bertellia's gentle smile conveyed a knowledge and certainty that prompted Carrie to knit her brows and swallow hard. Bertellia looked around the room. "It's so sterile here. Let's go for a walk."

And they were outside, walking a curving path around a small lake. White swans floated. Frogs sat on lily pads. A warm breeze ruffled their hair.

Carrie stumbled at the sudden transition, nearly falling.

Bertellia caught her arm. "You'll get used to that. Now, where were we? Oh, right, heaven, hell, judgement, fire and brimstone, all that. That is not part of our program. You still have much work to do. There may be a final reward, but I've never known anyone who got there. We *all* still have much work to do. Why people dream of sitting around on clouds, playing a harp, I have no idea. I would be bored silly before the first millennium passed. Here's a hard truth: most people on Earth can't face the fact that they don't know what comes after death. Eternal darkness? Recycling? Reward or punishment? No one knows, so they make up stories about it. The best storytellers are called prophets. People believe, and that makes them feel better."

Carrie looked down. She was wearing a robe similar to Bertellia's, though hers was not nearly so lovely. She stopped. "This is too much. I can't handle it."

"Of course you can. What else are you to do? Where else are you going to go if you can't handle this? Don't worry, you will acclimate soon enough."

I have my doubts.

Chapter Seven

Michael awoke once again in his childhood bed. He looked out his window at the rain-heavy clouds. *Looks like I'm here for the long haul this time. Thought I might wake up in a different time or place, but here I still am. Now what? And, for that matter, when exactly is this? What year? What time of year? Time to find some answers.*

He slid down off the bed. His feet had just touched the floor when the door to his bedroom pushed open and Michael jumped slightly. His hand involuntarily reached under the pillow for the knife.

"Oh, my, Michael, what are you doing awake already? You're never awake this time of day." Tess, his nanny of many years. Her hair was more gray than black and her face was lined, but still, she looked younger than the last time he had seen her. She had retired to Alabama in 1974.

I know I was a disappointment to her, even though she never said anything.

Tess had been the closest thing to a nurturing figure in his life. He felt a sudden urge. Without thought, he ran to her and threw his arms around her wide waist.

"Now, Michael, what's all this about? You haven't loved on me since you were a little fella. What's gotten into you this morning? Up on your own, now this?" While she spoke, she moved away from Michael and pulled clothes out of his dresser drawers and set them on the end of his bed. "Here now. You get dressed, and I'll go make your breakfast."

She started toward the door, but stopped when Michael said, "Thank you, Tess." She stood stock still for two beats before moving again.

"Miracles aplenty today. Yes indeed."

Why in hell did I do that? Because she was kind to me, even when I didn't deserve it.

Tess shut the door behind her and Michael pulled the knife out. He turned it over in his small, soft hands. *What to do, what to do? Take it back to the kitchen, then have to get it again every night?*

He knelt in front of the toy box and removed the firetruck, the Slinky, and some oversized blocks with letters painted on four sides. He put the knife at the bottom of the box, then piled the toys on top of it, hoping it looked as it had before.

Not a perfect solution, but it will do for now. Guess I don't want to leave any toys lying around, or Tess will find the knife and get worried. He twitched his mouth, a thoughtful look on his face. *Wait a minute. Toys? Toys. I'm going to be expected to play with toys. Jesus Christ.* He nudged the toy box with his foot. *What the hell am I going to do? Tess is not going to let me watch television all day.*

His eyes rose to the bookshelf above the toy box. A full set of L. Frank Baum's *The Wizard of Oz* books leaned against several Winnie the Pooh books and half a dozen *Little Golden Books.* He stood on tiptoe and pulled two of the *Little Golden Books* down: *The Poky Little Puppy* and *The Red Hen.*

Oh, come on! Not this shit. Do they give library cards to little kids? Goddamnit, I am going to have to figure something else out, or I'll go crazy.

From downstairs, he heard Tess's voice call up, "Michael, come on, you're going to be late for school!"

School? Oh, there's no fucking way I am going to spend the day cooped up with a bunch of kindergarteners. Or first-graders. Or whatever class I am supposed to be in.

Michael pulled on the clothes Tess had laid out for him—white shirt, khaki pants, dark socks—then looked at the pair of brown loafers at the end of his bed. *No way those fit. They've gotta be way too small.*

They fit.

Michael shook his head. *I am a full-grown man in a child's body.*

Downstairs, Michael found Tess in the kitchen. She had put a bowl of oatmeal with a pat of butter and a sprinkling of sugar on the kitchen table for him. He pulled the chair out to sit down and was dismayed to find a stack of phone books on the seat.

I'm not even tall enough to reach the table.

The kitchen was modern for the time, with spotless countertops and stainless steel edging. It hadn't yet been remodeled into the avocado greens and burnt oranges that Michael remembered from the future, which was now, somehow, his past.

With a sigh, Michael clambered up and sat down on the books. He was still barely able to see over the lip of the table. *I feel like Alice after she drank from the bottle. Whatever, I've got to eat.*

Michael picked up the spoon and dug in.

"Aren't you forgetting something, young man?" Tess asked.

Michael looked at her, perplexed.

"Your prayers?"

Michael said, "Oh, right. Sorry I forgot, Tess," then closed his eyes and pretended to pray. When he peeked at her through one squinted eye, Tess had hurried away to the counter, where she was packing his lunch.

"Hurry now," she said, glancing at the clock on the wall. The bus will be here in fifteen minutes, and you've still got to brush your teeth and run a comb through that hair.

Michael felt a rock in the pit of his stomach. He pushed the oatmeal away after only a few bites.

"Tess?"

"Yes, child, what?"

I don't feel so good. I think maybe I should stay home."

Tess bustled over to him and pressed the back of her hand to his forehead. She cocked her head and squinted at him. "I won't hear none of that, now. You go on, finish getting ready. I'll keep an eye out for the bus."

She always did have my number.

Michael eased off the chair, jumping the last few inches to the floor. He hurried upstairs, brushed his hair and teeth and was back down in less than five minutes.

"That was awful fast. Let me smell your breath."

Michael was repulsed but knew he was beaten. He dutifully opened his mouth, and Tess bent over and sniffed.

"All right. Don't want you thinking you can pull one over on Tess." She held out a child's winter coat. "Here. Put this on, and run on out and catch the bus. Hurry now."

Michael slipped the coat on, grabbed his lunch pail, which was solid red—no *Munsters* or *Beatles* lunch boxes in the Hollister house—and headed for the back door. There was a Caldwell's State Farm Insurance calendar hanging by the back door, turned to May 1966.

It was misting lightly outside, typical for Middle Falls. In many parts of the country, April showers bring May flowers. In western Oregon, April showers bring more May showers. Michael turned the collar of his coat up and trudged out to the street at the spot where, as best he remembered, he was supposed to catch the bus.

Oh, my God, I don't want to do this. If I skip school, I'll be found out. Maybe not today or tomorrow, but soon enough, so that won't work. I can't imagine spending all day with a bunch of retarded seven- and eight-year-olds. I can't just run away from home yet, though. I don't have any money, and there's no way I can survive while I'm trapped in this tiny little body. Shit. Oh my God, I'd give anything to be old enough to just get in a car and drive away. I don't care where, just anywhere but here.

Michael's thoughts were interrupted by the arrival of the number six bus, which pulled to a stop in front of him. The front tires of the bus hit a puddle in front of the curb, splashing water up and over his boots.

Perfect. A day spent with children and *soaking wet feet.*

With a sigh of resignation, Michael climbed up into the bus. The steps seemed very high to him.

Mr. Jenkins, the bus driver, ignored him. He was looking above his head, at a mirror that showed him the length of the bus. "Hey, you kids! Knock off the roughhousing, or I'll send a note home to your parents." A few of the eighth graders in the back sniggered, but the bus fell into something resembling quiet.

The bus was half full, which meant there were open seats to choose from. He saw two boys looking through a stack of baseball cards, but most of the other kids up front were just staring out the window like little zombies.

Can't go to the back. The big kids, the junior-highers, sit in the back. Little kids sit up front, where it's a little safer.

Michael bypassed the first empty seat and sat in the second, sliding toward the middle.

Maybe if the bus doesn't fill up, I won't have some first-grader sitting beside me picking his nose.

His luck held for the next two stops, but at the third, a pasty-faced boy with messy blond hair clambered on, walked to Michael's seat, and said, "C'mon, Michael. Scooch."

With an eye roll, Michael slid over and looked out the window, ignoring the boy.

He knows my name. I don't even remember him. This is going to be tough. I'm not even sure which grade I'm supposed to be in. Let's do the math. If this is May 1966, then I'm eight years old. Just finishing second grade, then. Perfect.

"You got your project done yet?" the blond boy asked. I'm gonna finish mine this weekend. I'm making a map of Central America, using clay. What are you doing? Volcano?"

Michael turned away from the window and glanced at the boy. He saw he was holding a piece of paper that read *Permission Slip* across the top. Below that was a name: Jack Bruner.

Jack Bruner, Jack Bruner. Nope. No memory of him whatsoever.

"Volcano? No, no. I'm attempting to replicate Gregor Mendel's experiments with genetics in sweet peas, specifically whether or not certain characteristics are dominant or recessive. I'm breeding rats instead of pea plants. I'm hoping to develop a rat that will eat all the other rats. Good luck on your clay map."

Jack looked at him blankly. Michael glared at him. Finally, Jack said, "Oh. Okay, that's great," and looked straight ahead. The next time the bus stopped to pick someone up, he moved to a different seat. Michael could hear him talking to another boy, saying, "Oh, you're making a volcano? Nifty."

Michael allowed himself a small smirk. *Gotta find my fun where I can, I guess.*

A few minutes later, the bus pulled up to the covered area and all the kids hurried off, with Michael purposefully trailing the pack.

Second grade. Mrs. Mayhew. She was a mean old bat, but at least I remember where the classroom was. This is going to be a long day.

Michael wandered the halls of Middle Falls Elementary while kids filed into their various classrooms. Just as the bell rang, he darted into his classroom, spotted an empty desk, and took a chance it was his. He opened the hinged top and peered inside. He saw cursive handwriting samples inside, with his name scrawled across the top.

Made it. One obstacle down, several million to go. But where did that paper come from? I didn't make it. Was there another little Michael here yesterday, working on his handwriting? If so, where did he go?

Mrs. Mayhew stood at her desk. She was thick from neck to toe, which made her head appear small for her body. She wore round spectacles pushed down to the end of her nose and a shapeless gray dress that might have once had a pattern on it, which had now faded into obscurity. Her face looked like an apple left out in the sun too long, complete with a crab-apple nose.

"Settle down, now," she said, though, aside from the scuffling of feet, no one was making any noise. "Last names A through J, over to the reading table. Everyone else, work on your math assignment on page twelve of your workbook."

Michael stood with six other children and moved to a low, sturdy table in the corner with books stacked in the middle. He spotted a boy in the back with wavy black hair. He was leaning back in his seat, whispering to the boy behind him.

Zack Weaver. You bastard. You and your damned stupid brother. Tommy has really got something coming to him, first chance I get. Michael chuckled to himself. *But, damn, if I'm only in second grade, then that little shit isn't even in kindergarten yet. Guess I'll have to wait a while to even that score.*

He walked by Zack on the way to the table, fixing him with a glare.

"Michelle Fartister," Zack said, with a smile that was so barefaced, Michael wanted to smash his face into the desk.

I forgot. He was the one who started that. God, I hate him.

When all seven children were seated around the kid-sized table, Mrs. Mayhew passed out copies of a book titled *Friends Old and New.*

"Jeffery, open the book to the first story, *The Lost and Found Tree,* and start reading aloud, please."

Oh, good Christ. Just kill me now. No. Wait. Don't. I'll just have to start over again. The only way out of this hell is apparently one day at a time. This is my punishment.

Six long hours later, Michael disembarked from the school bus, tired, frustrated, ready to kill something if an opportunity presented itself. He marched into the house through the back door and slammed it behind him, throwing his coat against the wall.

"Oh, no! Who is coming into my kitchen with that bad attitude? What happened to the little boy that hugged me and said 'thank you' this morning? Where did he go?"

Michael glared at Tess. She absorbed it with no reaction.

"I had a shit day at school, that's all."

Tess gasped. "Michael Hollister! For the sake of your hind end, I am going to pretend like I didn't hear you say that. If Mr. Hollister heard you say that, he'd tan your hide."

"Mr. Hollister can kiss my ..."

"Michael Scott Hollister! That's enough! You march right up to your room and stay there until I tell you to come out."

"Fine!" Michael stomped up the stairs, down the hall and into his room, slamming his door behind him.

Come on, come on. Gotta get ahold of myself. If I keep this up, I'll end up where I don't want to be—in a shrink's office three days a week and medicated out of my mind. Calm down.

Michael kicked off his shoes, climbed up on his bed and lay down, staring at the ceiling. Minutes later, he was asleep.

He opened his eyes to the touch of Tess's hand across his forehead.

"I guess when you told me you weren't feelin' right this morning, you weren't lying. You've never come home from school and laid down before. Are you hungry?"

Michael nodded.

"I made some chicken and dumplings for you. Your mother called and asked if I can stay late this evening. She and your father are going to some affair. Come on down and eat your dinner, then I'll make some popcorn and we can watch the television."

Tess smiled at him. She didn't close the door behind her.

Even when I bitch her out, she's still nice to me. Who else in my life was ever like that? No one.

When Michael got to the bottom of the stairs, the smell of chicken and dumplings surrounded him. His stomach growled. It had been a long time since that peanut butter and jelly sandwich and banana at lunch.

An hour later, he was stuffed full and sitting on the couch in what his mother called *the television room.*

The television set wasn't a new arrival in the Hollister house. Mr. Hollister had brought one home the year Michael was born. He liked to have the latest gadget and the best of everything in his house. The current television was one of the new color ones, in a cabinet that had a stereo on one end and a liquor cabinet on the other. It was the envy of everyone else on the block. Neither the television nor the stereo were turned on often, though. Mrs. Hollister liked a quiet house.

Michael sat down in the middle of the couch with a small bowl of popcorn in his lap. Tess sat beside him with her knitting, not paying any attention to the television, which was tuned to CBS. The opening montage of *The Wild Wild West* came on.

Hey, okay, not bad. I liked this show.

When the show was over, Tess stood and walked to the television, clicking it off. "All right, young man. I think that's enough of that kind of violence. Your parents would have my hide if they knew I let you watch that. Upstairs, into your pajamas, and say your prayers. I'll be up to say goodnight."

"You're kidding. It's only 9 o'clock."

"Don't act surprised by your own bedtime. Off with you now. March."

Michael laughed. "Okay, I'm going."

What else can I do?

Before he went upstairs, Michael veered into his mother's office. *Don't know why she ever needed an office. She never worked a day in her life.*

There was a small, neat desk against one wall, a two-drawer filing cabinet beside it. The desk had a calendar, blotter, and neat containers for pencils, pens, and paper clips. The calendar was marked with social occasions and fundraising benefits. There was a bookcase against the far wall. At eye level were Bible studies and self-help books, like *How to Win Friends and Influence People* and *The Power of Positive Thinking*.

Michael ran his fingers along the spines of those books. *Boring, boring. Super-boring.*

From his vantage point closer to the ground, though, he spotted several books stacked behind the ones that were spine-out. He pulled the front books out a few inches and grabbed one of the hidden books. It was a worn paperback with two women on the cover, a church spire rising behind them. The title read *Peyton Place.*

Hmmph. Better, but doesn't look like me.

He pulled out the second book. *Valley of the Dolls.* Michael heard Tess in the kitchen, washing the last few dishes, so he slipped *Peyton Place* back, grabbed *Valley of the Dolls*, and hustled upstairs. He threw his school clothes into the hamper in his room, then found some pajamas in the bottom drawer of his dresser and put them on. He slipped the book under his pillow.

He did not pray. Even with incontrovertible evidence of life after death, Michael never prayed.

Two minutes later, Tess came in, picked up a stray sock that had missed the hamper, ruffled Michael's hair, then flipped off the light, closed his door, and went downstairs.

Michael waited a few minutes to give Tess time to settle down into the comfy chair in the television room with her knitting, then crept across the room to his toy box, where he slid the knife out of its hiding place. Back in bed, he swapped the book and the knife, turned on the small light on the table next to his bed, and began to read.

Chapter Eight

C arrie and Bertellia sat on a bench beside a pond. A golden light emanated from above, warming their faces. Bertellia raised her face to it, soaking it in.

"Let's start at the beginning," Bertellia said. "The universe is large beyond imagination. It contains an almost infinite number of dimensions, many of which are nearly identical. Each time you took your own life, a new dimension was created."

"How is it possible that a single action by someone as insignificant as me could cause an entire new dimension? I can't believe that."

"That's the thing about reality. Whether we believe it, accept it, or deny it, it *is*. You may choose not to believe in gravity while on Earth, but the apple still falls. If it helps, think of a spider spinning its web. Now, think of yourself as that spider, and each new life, each dimension that was created to accommodate it, is a new strand."

Carrie blinked. Again, she touched her forehead in confusion.

Bertellia gestured toward a bench facing the lake. "On Earth, the many belief systems contain both truths and falsehoods. It is the way of things."

"Thanks for clearing that up."

Bertellia continued on. "There is no heaven, as you were taught about it. No hell. There is life, ongoing life. The indestructible force in the universe is the spark you carry within you. The essence of who you are. It's in all of us, and it is eternal. Congratulations. You have eternal life." Bertellia pulled her lips back from her teeth in what might have been a smile, but the effect was unsettling.

"But there is a God, right?" Carrie bit her lip, regretting the question as soon as the words escaped her lips.

"How do you mean? An Old Man with a beard, sitting on a throne, passing judgement? Or just an amorphous, omniscient, omnipotent being?"

Carrie looked away, into a horizon that never seemed to end. She had never liked being talked down to, and it felt as though that was all that had happened since she opened her eyes in this new place, wherever she was.

"There may very well be some being like that. I don't know. I suppose that what we call the Machine is the God you think of. It is the Creator. If there is another, I have not been privy to that presence. There have been rumors of the Being of Light, perfect light, for as long as we have been capable of thought." She shrugged, eloquently.

"You know I'm completely lost, right? If there's a test coming up, I'm going to flunk."

Chapter Nine

The next day was Saturday, so Michael knew Tess wouldn't be in. When he woke up, the house was still quiet. Michael hid both the book and the knife back at the bottom of the toy chest and went down the hall to the bathroom. The clock in the hall bathroom said it was 8:15.

Don't know what time they got in, but it must have been late. Michael had read until after midnight, but hadn't heard his parents' arrival. He had become absorbed in the story of the three women and their trials and tribulations, and had a difficult time putting it down.

Back in his bedroom, Michael hunted through his drawers for something that didn't look like school clothes. Five minutes later, he was dressed and downstairs, where the only sound was the ticking of the kitchen clock.

I think I might die of boredom if I don't figure out something to keep me occupied.

He found a pair of Keds by the back door and laced them up.

The clouds had parted and sunshine poured through the window.

The Hollister home sat on a lot just shy of an acre, which meant the backyard was enormous. It was surrounded by a low cedar fence painted the same sparkling white as the house. A greenhouse sat in one corner, the interior lined with potting shelves. There was a garden shed with large sliding doors, where the gardener kept the lawn mower and edger. At the rear of the yard was a sprawling oak tree with ladder steps built into its trunk, which led to a small tree house, also painted white.

I'll be damned. I'd forgotten about that. Something killed the tree and Father had it taken down, when? I think I was in fifth or sixth grade.

Michael walked under the tree and looked up at the underside of the structure. Neat rows of two-by-fours acted as a foundation, with plywood on top of that.

Professional job. Not something he did. He's never driven a nail in his life.

Michael tested the first step. It was rock steady. A few moments later, he stood on the small deck that circled the tree house. He pushed open the door, which creaked loudly as if it hadn't been opened in some time. The interior was empty, aside from a throw rug Mrs. Hollister had insisted be put in. She couldn't bear the idea of Michael sitting on dirty wood.

Michael nodded. *I can use this. A place to get away. I can't see either of them bothering to climb up here. Perfect.*

By the time his parents woke up, Michael had moved some pillows and blankets from the linen closet, several flashlights and lanterns from the garage, his copy of *Valley of the Dolls,* and a few of the other trashy novels his mother had hidden away.

This will do for now. Got to figure out a way to get a library card, though, so I can get something good to read. Well, and I've got to figure out a way to get to the library. It sucks being a kid. I'm at the mercy of everyone around me.

The tree house had a small window on the wall opposite the door, which allowed him to look down into the neighbors' yard on the south side. He remembered the Parkers lived there—an old couple who rarely left their house. He searched his memory, trying to remember who was on the north side, but came up empty.

I remember there were a few different people in and out of that house, but I can't remember who lived there when I was little.

Michael went back out and stood on the small circle of decking. The property to the north was overgrown, with a weeping willow tree acting as the centerpiece of the yard. Rhododendron bushes had grown into rhododendron trees and were taking over much of the yard.

There was a large wooden deck attached to the back of the house. With a start, Michael realized there was a man standing on it, in a pool of sunshine, wearing what looked like pajamas. He was moving in an odd, coordinated way, as though dancing with himself. At one point, the man struck a pose with one arm extended toward Michael, the other hand tucked against his chest.

Michael made eye contact with the man, who didn't appear to be embarrassed in the slightest to be seen dancing with himself in his pajamas. He gave an almost imperceptible nod to Michael, then continued on with his movements.

Hmmm. A weirdo in the neighborhood. Along with Father, that makes at least two.

Michael spent most of the rest of the weekend in his little tree house, only coming in to the house to eat or sleep.

Mr. and Mrs. Hollister didn't miss him.

Chapter Ten

"There are no tests here. Or, our entire existence is a test, depending on how you look at it," Bertellia said.

"Have I mentioned that listening to you feels like opening a series of fortune cookies?"

Bertellia ignored this. "Think of the universe as a series of layers," she said. "You were on one layer on Earth. Now you are on another. Simple."

"Nothing is simple. I lived my life, at least part of it, over and over. I became acclimated to the idea that I would start over each time I died, but this is going to take some getting used to. I thought I knew what was coming, if I ever got out of that infernal loop I was in. It sure wasn't this."

"You were a believer. The more strongly you believed, the longer it will take you to adjust. But as I mentioned, it doesn't matter if you believe in it or not—reality *is*. When you were a baby, your crib was your entire world, but as you grew older you realized there was more. In the same way, when you were on Earth, you looked at the universe through the tiniest pinhole. Now you have grown again, and you look at the universe through a keyhole, instead of that pinhole. "

"But you see it all?"

Bertellia shook her head. "Oh, no. The first step to real growth is accepting what you do not know. I might see the universe through a small window instead of your keyhole, but I am aware of how limited my vision is."

"Okay. For the moment, I'm going to forget about everything you're saying that I don't understand, which is pretty much everything. Now that I'm here, what do I do?"

"You have enough *Life Accumulation* to move on. In fact, you had enough several lifetimes ago, but you were stuck in the loop."

"I've noticed that you have a knack for answering questions in a way that tells me nothing."

"I could always go away and come back in a few millennia and see if you understand better then ..." Bertellia trailed off, her voice remote.

I suppose once you know you are truly eternal, there's not much more to threaten you with, is there? Behave, or we'll make you really bored for a really long time.

"What I mean is, what do I actually *do* here? Mow the lawn? Feed the swans? Sit around on a bench and contemplate my navel and all the inscrutable answers you give me?"

"If you'd like. Is that something that would appeal to you?"

"No."

"We all have work to do here to pull our own weight. I can train you for the Temporal Relocation Assignment Department, if you'd like. If not, I can pass you on to Rampartine. She can train you for the Cosmic Organization Group. It's the filing room for the known universe. Honorable work. Of course, everyone would like to be on the Karma Delivery Service, but there are rarely openings there. You'd be waiting half of eternity just to get an interview. You can also choose to be reborn on Earth, if you'd like."

Carrie considered. *Another life. New possibilities, but new ways to mess up. I am tired of the terrible things that happen on Earth. There is beauty, but so much ugliness. I don't want to spend another lifetime with self-induced amnesia, wondering what the answers are to the Big Questions. I don't want to take another ride on that merry-go-round.*

"Let's just continue on with the idea that I don't understand anything you are saying, but I hope I'll catch up later. If you want to train me for the Temporal ..." she trailed off uncertainly.

"Temporal Relocation Assignment Department. Earth Division, to be specific."

"Yes. That. If you want to train me for that, I'm willing. When do we start?"

"We already did, of course."

Chapter Eleven

Michael stayed up late into the night, either reading or staring at the light under the crack of his bedroom door. *I'll be goddamned if I'm going to let him catch me sleeping when he comes.* After midnight on Sunday night, his vigilance was rewarded. He heard quiet, slippered steps approaching, then pause outside his door. Michael pulled the knife out from under his pillow and slid it under his blanket. He wiped his sweaty hands on his pajamas, then gripped the handle again. He lay down and half-closed his eyes.

The door slid open. His father was silhouetted by the light down the hall. A thin man, he cast a long shadow into the room. He was in the same blue and gray striped pajamas he had been wearing when Michael had killed him so many times. That memory gave Michael strength.

Clayton Hollister stepped inside and closed the door behind him. He took half a dozen steps and stood beside Michael's bed.

I should just jam this knife right into his crotch right now. It would be delightful to see him fall to the floor, wondering what the hell just happened. But then, I'd have to start over again. I need to make it through this.

Clayton reached his hand out for Michael.

Michael sat straight up, surprising Clayton.

"Hello, Father. We need to have a talk. For once, I'm glad you've come creeping into my room like the pathetic pervert you are."

Clayton stepped back as if he had been slapped. "Michael!" His voice was a hoarse whisper. "Stop it!"

"No, you're going to stop it, *Father*. Here's the way it's going to be from now on."

Goddamn it, I hate the way I sound. My missing teeth make me lisp, and it's hard to sound tough when you're a lisping eight-year-old.

Michael cleared his throat and tried to pitch his voice in a lower register to keep the tremble out of it. "Here's the way it's going to be. You are never going to come back into my room again. If you need something, send Mother or Tess. Neither of them will try and fuck me. I can't say the same for you."

Clayton stepped forward, hissing, "Now just a goddamned minute, Michael. I'm your father. You will not speak to me like that." He reached toward Michael.

"Really?" Michael pulled the knife from under the covers. The blade reflected his night-light. "This says I can talk to you however I damn well want. We both know what you want to do to me. You've done it before, but you will never do it again. I'm small right now, but I won't always be. If you ever come back into my room for any reason, I will kill you while you sleep."

Like I've done before.

"So, if you ever want to have a good night's sleep again, if you don't want to have to sleep every night for the rest of your life with one eye open, don't ever come in here again. Go find some other little boy to diddle. I don't care. Just don't come back here."

Clayton opened his mouth to speak, but nothing came out. He closed it with a wet slap. He made a sudden lunge for the knife.

Michael was expecting it. He recoiled a few inches and slashed the knife forward. The razor-sharp blade sliced across the tips of two of Clayton's fingers. Blood spattered onto the carpet.

"Goddamn it!" Clayton jumped back, jammed his injured fingers under his armpit to stop the bleeding, then glanced over his shoulder to see if all was still quiet in the house. He lowered his voice. "Michael, you little shit. You don't have any idea what you're doing. You don't get to fuck with me."

"And you don't get to fuck me anymore, period. If you try, you'll end up with much worse than a little cut on your hand."

Clayton took a step toward him, but Michael flashed the blade again. Clayton stopped on a dime, his jaw muscles twitching violently. "You little shit. I will make you regret this." He turned and silently slipped out of the room.

As soon as the door clicked shut, Michael could no longer keep the tremor out of his hand. He dropped the knife onto the bed. Tears came, and he sobbed convulsively into his pillow, smothering the sound.

Chapter Twelve

One moment Bertellia and Carrie were beside a tranquil lake. The next, they were in an impossibly huge room, surrounded by other people.

Carrie was seated on a comfortable chair, the small desk in front of her empty except for a milky white cylinder.

Bertellia stood beside her. "This will be your work area."

"Wonderful. And what, exactly, is my work?"

"You will be assigned lives to watch over. They will all be from Earth, and you may be familiar with some of them from your own last life cycle. That often happens. However, they may all initially be strangers to you. I am not privy to how the assignment algorithms work."

"That seems pretty simple. Is this"—Carrie pointed to the cylinder in front of her—"like a television, then? I'm just supposed to watch what people are doing, like some kind of guardian angel?"

"No, and no. This is your pyxis. Yes, it allows you to see what is happening to those you watch over, but it does much more. Here." Bertellia touched the cylinder, and the milky white became translucent. She deftly moved her hand in an intricate movement, and a picture with depth and breadth appeared. A young woman, bent slightly, walked a dusty trail, carrying a stick across her shoulders with a water jug hanging from each end. She met another woman heading the other way, nodded and spoke. The words appeared in Carrie's head.

"She's speaking English?"

"No, and neither am I. It doesn't matter. You will always hear what people say in a language you understand. If you thought in Farsi, or Portuguese, you would be hearing that language. Now, watch."

Bertellia spun the cylinder counterclockwise at a slight angle. The woman stumbled, as though she had tripped over a rock that was not there. The left-side jug of water slipped off her stick and fell to the ground. It did not break, but most of the water spilled. The woman dropped her head. She looked back at the way she had come, calculating. She drew a deep breath, reattached the jug to the stick, and continued on the way she had been going.

"Did you do that?"

"I did."

"That's horrible! Why would you do that to her? Has she done something to you?"

"Me?" The tinkling, wind-chime laugh. "No, of course not. What could she possibly do to me? I just used her as an example."

"Then, why?"

"Our job is to *feed the Machine.* Emotion is the energy we watch and collect, using the pyxis. Did you see her? Anger, despair, resignation, all over something so small."

Carrie tore her eyes away from the picture of the woman walking and fixed Bertellia with a glare. "Emotion? So, it can be any emotion? Happiness, grieving, fear, anger?"

"Yes. It doesn't matter. They all move the needle of the Machine equally."

"And my job is to make bad things happen to them, so they will feel more emotion?"

"No, not at all. Keep this in mind: you will do much better if you do not attach yourself to outcomes. Remember. Everyone you watch over has eternal life, just as you do. They cannot be truly harmed. Think of it this way. If you were on Earth, watching your own children play in your backyard, and you knew with complete confidence that absolutely nothing could harm them, would you worry about whether they were playing tag, instead of hide-and-seek? Of course not. Anything that happens to them on Earth is temporary. In almost all cases, it is better to simply let your people live out their lives. Human beings manufacture enough pain, joy, and contentment on their own, every day. You rarely need to interfere. I simply wanted to show you what is possible. Initially, you will just watch and collect their emotions."

"Just watch," Carrie said, dully.

"And detach yourself from the outcome. Your job is to feed the Machine, not babysit. If you cannot learn that, you will not survive here. You will be recycled. Here," Bertellia said, lifting the pyxis and holding it out to Carrie. "You will need this."

Carrie reached out to accept it, but when she touched it, it wasn't the cylinder any more. It was a large book. The outside of the book read simply *Training Manual.*

Chapter Thirteen

The last week of school was an eternity for Michael. The hours ostensibly spent learning simple division or reading all over again were bad enough, but recess was worse. Michael had no close friends, and the truth was, he had never wanted any. He had no interest in playing tetherball or four square. But standing off by himself, quietly doing nothing, made him a target.

Monday of that last week of school was a blue-sky-and-sunshine kind of day in western Oregon, and the kids of Middle Falls Elementary moved out from under the covered play area to play freeze tag and football in the expansive school yard. Small groups of girls huddled together and talked about other small groups of girls.

Michael kept his hands in his pockets, eyes on the ground, and wandered the fringes, willing the time to pass. At one point, his path veered near a group of sixth graders playing touch football.

Greg Mylie, one of the earliest recipients of puberty in the school, was running with the football. Instead of running downfield, he veered left and plowed right over and through Michael, who went down in a tangled heap in the still-damp grass. As he stood up, Mylie ground his elbow into Michael's solar plexus, knocking the wind out of him and bringing tears to his eyes.

"Watch it, idiot! We're playing football. Stay out of the way, or I'll really run you over next time."

Michael picked himself up and looked down at the grass stains on his khakis. He brushed himself off and walked away without a word.

"You're such a weirdo. Stay out of the way next time," Greg said, laughing at Michael's retreating back, as he threw the football back in.

The rest of the football players laughed, happy that Greg had run over Michael instead of one of them.

Interminably, the final days of the school year passed and the last Friday arrived. Michael sat at his desk, tapping a pencil, waiting for the final bell that would free him from the burden of spending seven hours a day with children for the next three months. Every school day had been an exercise in eternity, but this Friday had been the worst. Report cards had been handed out, desks emptied and cleaned, and there were no more tasks on the school calendar.

That being the case, Mrs. Mayhew had the class play games like Heads Up 7-Up and Telephone.

Excruciating.

Michael refused to play, and the other children soon learned to skip him. This made everyone happier, including Mrs. Mayhew, who was in the last day of her long career and saw nothing but a happy retirement of crocheted doilies, evening fires, pots of tea, and Agatha Christie mysteries in her future.

Like all things both good and bad, the school day finally passed, and Michael carried his paper bag full of drawings and old papers with him to the bus. He glanced outside and saw that the buses were already idling. Children were laughing and cheering at the prospect of summer.

Michael glanced down at the paper bag. *There's no way I'm taking this shit home. No one would care.*

He ducked into the boys' bathroom, intending to dump the whole thing into the garbage and run to his bus. When he pushed the door open and hustled to the garbage can, he saw Greg Mylie go into the far bathroom stall. He paused, uncertain what to do with this opportunity.

A wet fart, followed by a deep burp, echoed off the tiled walls. Michael took a step back in revulsion.

Such a hillbilly heathen.

He turned to leave, but out of the corner of his eye, he spotted a mop bucket in the corner. He glanced inside and saw that it was half-filled with gray, filthy water. Several black hairs floated on the surface.

He took two steps toward the occupied stall and saw that Mylie hadn't even bothered to shut the door. That clinched it.

Michael snuck back to the bucket and hoisted it, testing its weight. *Yeah, I can do this.*

He crab-walked with the bucket between his legs until he stood in front of the stall. Mylie was absorbed in picking his nose up to the second knuckle. He pulled his finger out slowly, then flicked it toward Michael.

"What do you want, ya little shit-weasel? Another pounding? Get outta here."

Michael didn't speak, but picked up the bucket, pulled it behind him, and paused just long enough to enjoy the look of surprise on Mylie's face as he comprehended the inevitability of what was to come. The stinking water hit him in the face. Since he had opened his mouth to scream, it went down his throat, gagging him.

Michael waited long enough to imprint the piece of art in front of him—*young boy choking on mop water*—into his brain, then turned and ran.

Mylie didn't bother to waste his breath on threats. He jumped out of the stall, still choking and grasping at his sopping-wet pants as he did. When his feet hit the puddle of water, they shot out from under him and he landed flat on his back with a wet splat.

Michael laughed. "Perfect."

He ran from the bathroom and jumped onto his bus just as Mr. Jenkins put it in gear. He glued his eyes to the window and was rewarded with one last view of Greg Mylie as he emerged from the school doors, pants at half-mast, soaking wet from head to toe, cussing up a blue storm.

MICHAEL WOKE UP THE next morning as close to happy as he had been since arriving back in 1966. *At least I don't have to go to school. It'll be boring as shit around here, too, but I won't have to read another goddamned "Dick and Jane" book.*

He sat up in a bed, a lightning bolt of an idea striking him. *Holy shit, wait a minute. What if I start acing all their stupid tests, instead of holding back. I remember reading about some twelve-year-old kid who graduated from college. Maybe he wasn't a genius, but just someone like me. Maybe he knew he would rather die than spend all these years in grade school, so he did well enough on tests that they skipped him ahead. Maybe I can do that.*

With this new idea rattling around in his brain, Michael got dressed, found the strawberry Pop Tarts where Tess had left them, and climbed up to his tree house. He surveyed his back yard, where nothing was happening, aside from a squirrel watching him from the bird feeder, and an obnoxious Steller's jay squawking at him for no particular reason. Then he spotted the old man next door, dancing with himself in his pajamas.

Michael stood on his small balcony and stared at the man. He was short and squat, yet moved with a certain grace. He had gray hair and eyebrows so bushy Michael noticed them across the distance. He wore black glasses and flowing Asian robes.

Soon enough, the man noticed Michael and lifted a hand in recognition.

Slowly, Michael extended his hand toward him and raised his middle finger.

The man laughed so hard he bent over double. When he straightened up, he gave Michael his own one-finger salute, but he was still smiling. He shook his head, then returned to his odd exercise.

Interesting. A little kid flips him off, but he doesn't go crazy. I thought he might stomp inside and call my parents, but instead, he just laughed.

Michael munched his Pop Tarts and turned his mind to his biggest challenge—how to kill time over the summer. A smile came over his face. He stuffed the rest of his breakfast into his mouth and hurried down the ladder. He cautiously opened the door to see if anyone else was awake yet, but the house was still quiet.

Michael crept into the cavernous garage. His father's Cadillac and his mother's Chrysler were in their appointed spaces. The Hollisters drove American—good Detroit steel—of course. *Wish I had my Karmann Ghia back. That was a sweet ride. Eventually I will.*

In the far corner were some of the abandoned toys of the household. The old refrigerator from the kitchen stood sentry, still operating, though it was empty. There were piles of tarps and unused camping equipment stacked on broad wooden shelves.

When in holy hell would my parents have gone camping? Was it some kind of company-wide retreat or something? I can't picture either of them sleeping on the ground in a sleeping bag.

Michael lifted the tarps, launching a cloud of dust into the air.

I know it's around here somewhere. This is where we always kept it. Aha!

Behind a box, Michael found what he was seeking—a tiny little television with a white earpiece cord wrapped around it. It had a four-inch screen.

Perfect for the tree house. Now, for electricity.

More digging produced several outdoor extension cords that together would be long enough to reach the tree house.

Father will never sign off on this, so I'm going to have to be clever.

Michael ran the television out and up into the tree house, then retrieved the extension cords. He plugged the end of the first into the outlet on the side of the house, then strung it along the edge of the flower beds, where it couldn't be seen from inside the house. He strung it up the back of the tree and into the tree house, then ran back and buried the cord under a few inches of soil.

He plugged the tiny television in, and a small, white dot in the center of the screen grew to a snowy, wavy picture. He pulled the rabbit ears out and moved them one way, then the other. The picture eventually became a little clearer. It was so small he had to almost squint to see it. It was black and white, but it was substantially better than the options he'd had at the beginning of the morning, which had been none.

Unnoticed, Clayton Hollister stood at the kitchen window, drinking a cup of coffee and watching Michael's labors.

Michael sat down on the folded blanket in the corner of his tree house. *Not exactly the Fortress of Solitude, but not bad. It's dry, away from everyone else, and I've got a few things to keep me from going crazy with boredom.*

He tuned the television to channel six and found a cartoon—*The Secret Squirrel Show*. He flipped it to channel eight, where *The Flintstones* was playing.

"Well, shit," Michael mumbled. *Maybe the TV wasn't a great idea after all.*

He heard a steady snip-snip-snip from outside and poked his head out.

The odd neighbor next door was working just below him, on the other side of the fence, trimming some bushes. He had traded in his robe for more conventional old-man clothes—blue shorts held up by a black belt above his navel, a checked shirt, and dress shoes with blue socks pulled up to his knees.

Michael watched him for a moment, then, pitching his voice so that it carried across the fence, offered, "Might use those shears on your eyebrows instead. They need it worse than that bush."

The man continued on—snip, snip, snip—as though he hadn't heard anything. After a few moments, he set the pruning shears down, pulled a handkerchief out of his back pocket and wiped sweat off his face.

"There's some truth in what you say. Still, I rather like my eyebrows. I'm not fond of this bush."

He went back to work. Snip-snip-snip.

Michael shook his head. *What does it take to insult this guy? Is he too stupid to know when someone is making fun of him?*

Michael dropped down from the tree house and went to the flower bed, where he pushed some more soil over the extension cord.

"Are you interested in a little manual labor, my boy?"

Michael didn't hesitate. "How much you paying?"

"How about a firm handshake and the knowledge of a job well done?"

"How about you blow it out your ear?"

"Youths, today. Always focused on the almighty dollar. All right, I'll make you this deal. If you do a suitable job, I'll pay you a dollar."

A dollar. Whoopee. Still, a dollar in 1966 buys a lot more than it did in 1977. Gotta start somewhere.

"Can I see the bush?"

"Of course. Any good worker wants to understand the scope of a bid before accepting a job. Use the gate in the middle of our fences. I believe there must have been a time when people who lived in our houses liked each other, to have put that gate in."

"Must have been before we moved here. My father doesn't like anyone."

Michael opened the gate and looked at the old man. Behind him, a pile of limbs spread on the ground.

"Tell you what, mister. I'll trim it all the way to the ground and put all the branches into a pile for you to burn for two dollars."

"That's not necessary. I don't love this bush, which aspires to take over my entire yard, but I have no need to murder it. If you'll just cut it back to behind the surrounding bushes, then stack the residue at the very back of the yard, I'll pay you a dollar and a half."

"Whatever. I need the money, so I'll do it."

"Got a bubble gum habit you need to feed?"

Michael fixed him with a glare. "Nope. Heroin. My dealer insists on cash, and I'm a buck fifty short."

The man tipped his head back and laughed. The sound echoed around the yard. When the laughter passed, he looked at Michael shrewdly. "I think you are not what you present yourself as, are you lad? What's your name?"

Michael considered saying "Luke Skywalker," but said "Michael," instead.

"Michael, my name is Jim Cranfield. Here are the tools of your trade," he said, handing the pruning shears off.

The shears were a little big for his hands, but by holding them in the middle, he managed to make them work. He set to snipping away the branches and soon lost himself in the work. *Kind of nice to have something to do, instead of just waiting for time to pass.*

Half an hour later, the bush was pushed well back into its proper boundaries. He looked around for Cranfield, found him sitting at a table in the sun on his back deck, sipping on a can of something or other. Cranfield waved him over.

When Michael set the trimmer down on the deck, he felt a pain in his right palm. He looked down to see the beginnings of a small blister.

"Come on, Michael, sit down and have a Coke. Your mother won't care if you have a Coke, will she?" He pushed a small bottle of Coca-Cola across the table toward him.

"My mother only cares where her next happy pills are coming from. As long as the doctor keeps those coming for her, she doesn't give two shits where I am."

"So that explains your rather adult vernacular as well, then. In any case, here's a Coke to celebrate a job well done."

Cranfield reached his hands out, letting them hover over the table for a moment. He turned them this way and that, so Michael could see they were empty. His fuzzy eyebrows lifted, a silent plea to watch carefully. When he turned his hands over again, each had three quarters in them. He passed his left hand over his right, and all six were neatly stacked. He placed them on the patio table with a small grin.

Michael nodded his thanks for the small magic show and scooped the money off the table. "Can I ask you a couple of questions?"

Jim nodded.

"Why do you think an eight-year-old is going to understand words like 'vernacular'?"

"Do you understand it?"

Michael nodded.

"There you are. I don't assume that all children are incapable of understanding. What else?"

"How come I see you dancing with yourself?"

"Ah. That is not dancing. It is tai chi chuan, sometimes called *the ultimate of ultimates*. It is a form of a discipline I learned in Taiwan many years ago. It is good for this old body."

"It looks weird."

"As do so many things to people who do not understand what they are looking at."

"I've got to go."

"Yes, of course, your heroin dealer awaits."

Michael granted him something close to a smile and went back to his tree house, where he stashed his money. He turned the television on again, hoping for something other than kids' cartoons. Channel eight was playing a gardening show, but when he flipped to channel six, he saw a movie was playing. It was one he had seen before, but it took him a few minutes to recognize it.

Two Roman centurions were on horseback, making an announcement of some sort. Michael turned up the volume just in time to see Tony Curtis jump to his feet and say, "I'm Spartacus."

Of course. Pretty good movie. No idea why a group of men would offer to die to save someone else, though. I'd just point at Kirk Douglas and say, "Here you go. Can I go back to work now?"

THE FIRST TWO WEEKS of summer vacation dragged, but life was better when Michael didn't have to deal with the children of Middle Falls Elementary. He had fallen into a set schedule—wake up early, eat whatever breakfast Tess made for him, then be out in the tree house before his father came downstairs. He spent his day either in the tree house, reading and watching television, or sitting on Jim Cranfield's back porch.

Michael didn't trust him, of course, because he trusted no one. He did find him amusing, though, and Cranfield was the only person who had ever treated him like something other than a kid, so he found himself spending more and more time with him.

Sitting on the back porch again one sunny afternoon, Michael asked, "What do you do for a living? You never go to work. Did you kill your wife and live off the insurance now?"

"I kill many, many people, but I have no fear of arrest. I am a writer. Not an author, nothing that highfalutin, but a writer. I write what people call pulp fiction. I just happen to be somewhat successful at it."

"What's that?"

"Pulp fiction is the stuff people actually want to read, not the stuff they're told they should read."

"Really? Tell me something you've written."

"I write a series of books about a hero called The Magician. He uses sleight of hand and illusions to solve crimes. The first one is called *Abracadaver*. The second is *Hocus Corpsus*. You get the idea."

"Can I read one?"

"Wouldn't you rather read something more enlightening? Like the back of a cereal box?"

Michael shook his head.

Jim sighed, stood, and went inside. A minute later, he returned with a paperback book in his hand. The cover showed a tall, handsome magician with a thin black moustache, waving a wand over a prone, floating woman wearing a colorful costume. Large, bright red letters proclaimed, "Abracadaver!" Below that, in equally bright yellow letters: "The Magician, Volume One."

"I have a hunch that if your parents find that, they'll throw it in the trash. According to the critics, that's where it belongs." He appeared unfazed by whatever critical drubbing he might have received. "Think you can read that?"

"Yep."

"So be it. Let me know if you want to trade it for something better. I have a full library in the house. You might like some of my Robert Heinlein books, like *Have Space Suit, Will Travel.*"

Michael shook his head slightly.

Still not sure about you. I think I'll stay out here where it's safe.

"Okay. See ya." Michael jumped through the open gate, slamming it closed behind him, and ran to his tree house. One minute later, he was lost in the macho world of *The Magician.*

Simeon Mantoni was the magician, and he was able to use sleight of hand and misdirection to get him out of every jam, to rescue every attractive woman, and to deal with every wrong, quickly and with no feelings of remorse.

Michael read *Abracadaver!* in a single afternoon. He finished it just as Tess called him in to supper. He was dismayed to find that this was to be a family dinner, a rarity in the Hollister household. His mother and father were already sitting at the table, waiting for him.

"Michael," his mother said, "why don't you say grace for us."

Michael rolled his eyes slightly, but not enough to attract the attention of his father. He bowed his head, steepled his hands in front of him and said, "Bless us, oh Lord, and these thy gifts, which we are about to receive from thy bounty."

"Amen," his mother said, pleased that he had gotten through it without a stumble. She rewarded him with a tightly frozen smile, then began dishing roast beef and au gratin potatoes onto her plate. She passed the dishes on to Clayton Hollister, who had set the *Wall Street Journal* up in front of him.

"Must you?" she asked, through the same glacial smile.

Clayton read on until he had finished the article, sighed, folded the paper and set it off to the side. He gazed off into space somewhere above Michael's head.

The rest of the meal was silent, aside from the clicking of forks and scraping of knives.

Finally, Michael said, "May I be excused?"

"Going back out to your tree house?" his mother asked. "It seems like you'd live out there if you could. I don't see the attraction. I'm sure it's dirty, and there must be spiders and God only knows what else out there."

Michael just shrugged and said no more. *Don't argue. Don't defend. Get out quick.*

She sighed. "Fine, I don't care."

Michael retreated from the dining room. Just as he closed the kitchen door, he heard his father say, "Don't worry, I'm about to take care of that problem."

Chapter Fourteen

Carrie opened the training manual. It reminded her of her grand-mother's Bible, with a heavy leather cover and onionskin pages. The first page contained two sentences: *It will be all right in the end. If it's not all right, it's not the end.*

"Okay ..." Carrie mumbled to herself. She glanced up. All around her, other students were hunched over their own copies of the manual. One thin woman with long, jet-black hair was flipping through the pages as though she was at a speed-reading class.

"There's one in every group," Carrie muttered to herself.

She turned to the second page. Another few words: *Life is not a race. Not a marathon, not a sprint. Life is. Nothing more.*

"What the heck? Does this book respond to my questions?" She turned the page.

Yes. No. Maybe.

"Uhn," Carrie said in frustration. "Does everyone and everything in this place talk in riddles?" She turned the page.

Yes. No. Maybe.

Carrie shut the manual with a dull thud, then took a deep breath. She looked around and saw that everyone else in the room was studying their manual industriously. *I just have to ask the right questions. Okay. Will you teach me what I need to do my job here?* She opened the book again, but did so more than halfway through.

Only two words on the page: *Of course.*

Holy crap, a straight answer. Now I'm getting someplace. What, exactly, is my job? She turned the page.

The longest answer yet: *Every job, every undertaking, is what you make it. Your task is to follow the luminous path. When darkness is all around you, it is easy. When the light is intense, it becomes more difficult.*

And, we're back to the fortune cookies, Carrie thought. *This is going to take some doing.*

Chapter Fifteen

The next morning, Michael slipped out of his room quietly, a little before 7 a.m., when his father would typically still be in the shower or getting ready for work. When he walked into the kitchen looking for breakfast, though, he was surprised to find his father, dressed in one of the dark suits he wore to work, standing at the back door with a cup of coffee in his hands. A happy, satisfied look sat, unaccustomed, on his face.

Michael followed the direction of his stare. Two men were at the back of the yard, dismantling his tree house. A third was pulling up the power cord he had run so carefully along the edge of the garden, looping it over his arm as he went. A fourth man stood by, oiling a chainsaw.

"Unnnh," was all Michael could say, a word that meant, "I can't believe you'd actually do this," and, "But of course you would," and "Fuck you, too, Dad," all in one single syllable of frustration.

Father and son created a frozen tableau, staring out the back door at the workmen industriously tearing the tree house apart, board by board. After a moment, Clayton turned his head and looked at Michael, with the eyes of an eagle closing in on a rabbit in the field below. He set his coffee cup down on the kitchen counter, nodded down, and said, "Michael," then walked out the front door.

Michael slammed through the back door and stood on the porch steps. *What chance have I got against him? He's full-grown. I'm a kid again. If I tell people what he's done, it's just my word against his, and who is everyone going to believe?* Michael balled his small hands into fists at his side. *Shit! Oh, my God, I hate him so much!*

Michael approached the workman with the chainsaw.

"Whatcha doin'?" Michael said, doing his best to appear as if he really were an eight-year-old boy.

"Gonna cut this tree down, kid."

"Why?" Michael asked, although he was sure he already knew the answer.

"'Cuz that's what the man is paying us to do."

Michael knew the six quarters he had stashed would never be enough of a bribe to stop the dismantling and destruction of the tree house and tree. He walked among the scattered remains of the tree house—boards, the old carpet, his stash of books. He grabbed the copy of *Abracadaver* and left the rest behind.

They can burn Mom's trash books if they want to. I don't care.

He tucked the book under his arm and pushed through the gate to Jim Cranfield's yard. It was empty, with no sign of the older man anywhere. He looked hopefully up at the deck, but it was empty. Michael's shoulders sagged.

He tentatively walked up the steps to the deck and sat down at the small table and chairs. He set the book on the table, then drummed his fingers.

A minute later, Jim Cranfield came out, drying his hands on a dishrag.

"Young Master Hollister. Good morning." He glanced at the activity across the fence and said, "It is a day filled with foreboding and bad tidings, especially if you are inclined to want to while away your hours in a tree house."

"My father is a raging asshole in more ways than you can ever know."

Cranfield nodded, pursed his lips, but remained silent.

"The only reason he's taking it down is because he knows I like it. He'll do anything he can to get rid of something I like." To his dismay, Michael felt tears forming in his eyes. He angrily wiped the back of his hand across his eyes. He took a deep, shuddering breath.

Shit. What is it about being a kid that makes it so easy to cry?

Michael shrugged. "Well, there isn't anything I can do about it, so I guess I might as well forget it. I'll spend the rest of the summer locked in my bedroom." He shoved the book across the table. "Thanks. I finished it. Can I have the next one?"

"Already?"

Michael nodded.

Cranfield stood, plucked the book off the table and disappeared into the house. A moment later, he reappeared, holding a small stack of trade paperbacks. On top was a slim volume called *Hocus Corpus – The Magician, Volume Two*. Michael riffled through the lurid covers and saw more titles like *Prestidigitlesstation, Clairavoidance,* and *Spell-BOUND*, which featured a beautiful woman tied securely to a chair.

"That won't make up for your lost tree house, but it might help you kill a few hours, not to mention a few brain cells."

"Thanks," Michael said, eyes downcast. "Well, guess I better go. Thanks for the books. I'll take good care of them."

"Excellent. We should strive to take care of all books, even ones with pedigrees as mongrel as those."

"You're so weird."

"Duly noted. Now, if you'll excuse me, I have to attend to my kombucha."

I have no idea what that is, and I don't even think I want to ask. What a weird old dude. Still, nice guy. He takes time to talk to me, even though he thinks I'm just a little kid.

Michael scooched his butt forward so he could hop down from the patio chair and crossed back through the fence into his yard. He looked up just as the man with the chainsaw put a belt around the tree and began to climb. When he got to the top, he fired up the chainsaw, and the sound echoed around the neighborhood. He cut off several small branches at the top, worked his way down twenty feet or so, then cut through the main body of the tree, which fell harmlessly into the yard.

Makes sense, I guess. If they had just felled it where it was, it might have been tall enough to reach the house. And I would have stood here and laughed my ass off. The only thing better would have been when Father came home to survey the damage.

Michael stopped in his tracks. *Wait a minute. I'm too small to knock a tree down on the house, but that doesn't mean I am helpless.*

Michael pushed through the back door, ignoring Tess as she said, "Hello, Michael," with a worried expression on her face.

She knew how much I loved being out there. Good to know someone in this house cares about me.

He strolled through the dining room and into his father's office. He rarely went into the office because it felt like his father was everywhere inside that room. It even smelled like him, or his cologne, at least. A large mahogany desk sat in the middle of the room, with a high-backed leather swivel chair behind it. Low-wattage bulbs burned in lamps set in the corners of the room. The walls were covered with pictures of Clayton Hollister, one of Middle Falls' leading citizens, accepting awards from the Kiwanis, the Lions, and the Chamber of Commerce. There was a picture of him shaking hands with Governor Mark Hatfield, and one shot of him posing with a swordfish, taken somewhere in Mexico. The wall behind the desk was empty, except for one frame, perfectly centered. That frame was almost empty as well, with only a small rectangle in the middle. Michael didn't have to look at it to know what it was—the Inverted Jenny stamp. It might not be the very rarest stamp in the world, but it was close. A small lamp hung over the frame, shining a subtle light down on the tiny red and blue stamp with the upside-down airplane on it.

Michael knew the story of the stamp only too well. How it had been handed down from his grandfather to his father and how, someday, it would be given to him. He knew that Clayton Hollister loved that stamp more than he loved anything, certainly including his family.

I wonder what it's worth? Doesn't matter, because I know what it's worth to him. Every time some guy in a suit comes to the house, he drags him in and shows it to him, whether he wants to see it or not.

Michael peered closely at the stamp under the frame, which had been professionally mounted under museum-quality glass. The frame hung from a strong wire attached to closed-eye hooks, which were sunk into studs in the wall.

He sure doesn't want anything to happen to it, does he?

Michael reached up and tugged on the frame, but it held firm. He pulled harder, with no result. Finally, he let all his weight dangle off it, but it clung stubbornly to the wall.

Shit!

He looked around to see if Tess had been alerted that he was somewhere he wasn't supposed to be, but he was still alone. He glanced at the desk and saw a paperweight designed to look like Mount Rushmore.

He picked it up, measured the heft. Michael was never going to be an athlete, even when he was fully grown, but at that moment, he made the pitch of his life. He wound up and threw the paperweight from three feet away, smashing it directly into the frame. The museum glass didn't shatter into a million pieces, but rather, with a huge bang, broke in large shards and fell to the carpeted floor.

Michael glanced over his shoulder again. *Only got a second now.*

The frame still hung on the wall, swaying slightly at an angle. Michael picked a large piece of glass away from the middle of the frame, reached in and peeled the stamp away from the backing. He held it close for just a moment, savoring it.

Then, he tore it in half. And half again, and a third time. He tried to tear it in half a fourth time, but it resisted the strength of his small fingers. He shrugged, stacked the eight pieces of the stamp neatly in the middle of the blotter on the desk, then leaned over and carefully spit a loogie on the pile.

"Michael! Oh my stars, what have you done? What is Mr. Hollister going to do when he sees this?" Tess's eyes were wide with shock and surprise.

Michael, still bent over the desk after spitting on the remains of the stamp, glanced up at her, a devilish grin playing on his lips.

"I. Don't. Care."

Tess's hand flew to her mouth. She had never heard such blasphemy in the Hollister home. "Oh, Michael," she said softly, "have you lost your mind?"

"No." Michael held her gaze for a long moment. "Tess, do you know what my father has done to me?"

Tess took a step toward Michael. A shadow of concern, long buried, flitted across her eyes.

Michael saw her expression and seized on it. "Ah, so you *do* know. No, wait. That's not right. You *suspected,* maybe, but you never had enough information. Of course not. He only came into my room in the middle of the night, when Mother was so drugged that an earthquake could have shaken the house off its foundations and she wouldn't have woken up."

"Michael! You sound ... so ... different. So much older."

You don't know the half of it.

"Where's Mother?"

"She ... she's upstairs."

"Asleep again, slumbering in Morpheus's arms, thanks to a few of her pills, no doubt. She must have taken a handful not to have heard that crash." Michael glanced over his shoulder at the skewed frame and smiled again, with a contented look that chilled Tess. "You should probably call Father and let him know he needs to come home. He's not allowed in my room any more, but I'll wait for him in the television room."

Tess, stunned into silence, started to ask what "not allowed in my room" meant, but changed her mind and hurried to the kitchen. She picked up the phone. Michael could hear the repeated twirling of the rotary dial. Then, in a panicked tone he'd never heard from her lips: "Mr. Hollister, please. This is his housekeeper."

Michael walked into the next room and clicked the television on. A black and white movie was playing, but Michael couldn't focus on it. He was too antsy—he knew there would be hell to pay. He walked over to the stereo cabinet and thumbed through the records inside. *Sing Along With Mitch, Even More Sing Along with Mitch, Nighttime Sing Along with Mitch.*

Come on, Dad. It's 1966. No Nat King Cole or the Kingston Trio, even? Are they a little too black, or a little too hippy for you?

Michael sat down on the couch and stared off into space.

Now what, Father?

At first, adrenaline coursed through his veins and he sat bolt upright.

I'll bet it won't take him long to get home once he finds out his precious stamp has been ruined. I want to see the look on his face when he actually sees it.

Michael's expectation of a quick resolution came and went. The grandfather clock in the corner ticked away the seconds, the minutes, an hour. The pendulum swung back and forth in a stately motion, lulling Michael into sleep.

Michael awoke two hours later to the sound of muffled voices in the kitchen. He had fallen over against the arm of the sofa but sat up quickly, trying to clear the sleep cobwebs from his head. After destroying the stamp, he had felt elated at first about striking such a telling blow in retaliation. Now, several hours and an intervening nap later, his stomach was tossing and turning, and regrets were already beginning to form.

He listened intently, but could only pick up snippets of his father's voice. "... had to pull a lot of strings ... not even open during the summer ... the last damn straw ... no son of mine ... if he even *is* my son ..."

Michael did his best to focus and regain his composure, but sleep clung to his brain. He took a deep breath, pulled his hand back and struck himself as hard as he could across the right side of his face. A red print rose immediately, and he heard a slight ringing in his ears, but his eyes focused again.

Steps echoed across the tile floor of the kitchen, then muffled into the deep carpeting of the dining room, and then entered the television room.

Michael expected to be confronted with anger, hatred, probably violence. He was unprepared for the calm and cool Clayton and Margaret Hollister who stood in front of him. His mother still looked as sleepy-drunk as Michael had been a few moments before.

The bastard actually looks calmer than normal. That can't be good.

"Michael, after what you did," Clayton said, glancing toward his office, "there will be no further discussion. You have forfeited the right to live the good and easy life we have provided you."

"Including slipping the dick to me every chance you got?"

Margaret Hollister gasped, but before that sound faded, Clayton bridged the distance and slapped Michael hard enough to knock him out of the chair.

Clayton's breath came in ragged puffs. Fury blazed in his eyes. He straddled Michael, leaned close and whispered, "That's enough. Do you understand?"

"Clayton! He's just a boy!"

"I'm not sure what he is any more, but I don't think it's a boy. In any case, it's not our problem now." He looked down at Michael, who had a red welt on both cheeks. "Go pack your clothes. Tess put a suitcase on your bed. I'm putting you out."

Michael picked himself up. Inside, a battle raged. He didn't want to ask, but curiosity won out. "Where?"

A slow smile spread across Clayton's face, but of course it wasn't a smile at all—it was a baring of teeth. It made Michael shiver involuntarily. "Hartfield Military Academy. They might not be able to fix you, either, but they know what to do with boys like you. One way or the other, they'll solve this problem."

Chapter Sixteen

Michael didn't sleep that night. He had a terrible foreboding that his father would try to make one last nocturnal visit, so he sat on the edge of his bed, the same kitchen knife he had used to kill him dozens of times held loosely in his hands.

The hours passed, but no shadow darkened his door. By the first light of dawn, he was up and dressed. His father had told him that a taxicab would be at the house at 10:30 to take him to the bus depot.

Can't even bother to get rid of me by taking me to the bus themselves. Fine. I don't need them—or anybody. I'll be glad to be away from here.

He dressed in summertime clothes—a pair of tan shorts, white socks, and a blue pullover knit shirt—slipped on his Keds and pulled the small stack of books out from under his bed, where he had stashed them the day before.

He made his way downstairs and found bright sunshine streaming in through the kitchen windows, but no sign of Tess. Unusual for a weekday.

He opened the back door and stepped onto the porch. Immediately, his eye was drawn to the stump of the tree that had held his tree house twenty-four hours earlier.

Screw you. I'm glad I did it.

He walked through the dewy grass and pushed through the gate to the yard next door, hoping that Jim Cranfield would be up, enjoying a morning cup of coffee on his back deck. Instead, all was quiet.

Michael set the pile of books down, then clambered awkwardly up into the chair facing the sliding glass door. He plucked the top book off the pile and opened it just past the midway point.

Maybe I can at least finish this one.

He opened it to page sixty-seven.

Simeon checked the revolver in his front pocket, the one that was intended to be found. He gave a light pat under his left arm to make sure the small single-shot gun, the one intended to be easy to miss in a quick frisk, was in place. "They said to come unarmed, doll," he said to Bridge. If that's not a reason to carry at least two guns, I don't know what is. Now come here, and give me one of those special goodbye kisses. If I'm going to end up looking down the barrel of a gun, I want to do it with the taste of your lips fresh in my mind."

Twenty minutes and two dozen pages later, the slider whooshed open and Cranfield poked his head out. His graying hair was askew and stuck out at odd angles, as did his bushy eyebrows. "A little early for one of our visits, isn't it, Michael? You can't tell me you read all of those already. I know you're smart, but you haven't taken the Evelyn Wood speed-reading course, have you?"

"They're sending me away. I didn't want to take your books, or leave them to be found in my bedroom, so I brought them back." Michael closed the book he was reading with a slight regret—The Magician was in a terrible predicament, and Michael couldn't figure out what kind of magic he was going to work to escape.

"That's very responsible, Michael." Cranfield pulled his bathrobe tighter around himself, covering the white T-shirt and pale blue boxer shorts beneath it. "I have many copies of them, though. Are you sure you don't want to take them with you?"

Michael shook his head. "I'm not sure what it will be like where I'm going. Your books might be contraband there."

Cranfield cocked one great eyebrow. "Where are you off to, then?"

"Hartfield Military Academy. I'm not even sure where it is."

"Hartfield, Hartfield ... hmm. Hold on, I'll be back." With a flourish of his tartan robe, he disappeared back into the house. A few moments later, he re-emerged with a large book. He placed it on the table, took a seat, and patted the nonexistent pockets at the breast of his bathrobe.

Michael pointed to the top of Cranfield's head, where a pair of reading glasses perched.

"Oh, yes, there they are. Getting old is not for the faint of heart. They say the memory is the first thing to go, but I can't remember what is the second thing." He glanced at Michael over the top of the glasses, but Michael's expression didn't change. "This is not a morning for jokes, is it, young Master Hollister? You are correct." He flipped the book open to the very back, turned a page, then another, then ran his finger down a column until he found what he was looking for. "Mmm-hmm," he mumbled under his breath, then flipped back to a midway point in the book.

He looked at Michael again. "Just because I am a hack doesn't mean I can't be a factually accurate hack. I have a research library slightly better than what is available at the Middle Falls Library tucked away in what was once the spare bedroom. It serves several purposes—keeping me informed and keeping overnight company away. Can't say which I appreciate more. Now ..." He lowered his eyes to the book once again, and said, "Hartfield Academy, located in the tiny hamlet of Jenkins Cove, California, fifteen miles north of Crescent City. Hartfield Academy has prepared young men to serve their country in every conflict since World War I. It was founded by Curtis M. Hartfield in 1909 and is currently overseen by his grandson, Curtis M. Hartfield III. Hartfield Academy accepts boys for training between the ages of eight and eighteen years old."

Michael nodded. *I'll be the smallest one there, then, locked in with a troop of GI Joe wannabes. Thanks, Dad.*

Cranfield's eyes softened. "Well, that's probably not ideal, but there are worse scenarios for you, yes?"

"If he could have arranged to drop me into the Bataan Death March or the Trail of Tears, I'm sure he would have chosen one of those."

Cranfield smiled, but not with much humor.

Michael slid down off the chair and extended his small hand. "Thanks. You've been one of the less awful parts of this whole experience."

"High praise indeed," Cranfield answered, shaking Michael's hand. "Come see me when you come home for Christmas break, perhaps."

Part Two

Chapter Seventeen

The bus rattled and bumped as the driver shifted gears on the on-ramp to Interstate 5 southbound. Michael sat a third of the way back on the bus. He had chosen that seat because when he climbed aboard, that section was empty. He was hoping for no human contact for the rest of the day. His hopes were dashed when a skinny man with long, dishwater-blond hair, dressed in an orange tank top and bell-bottom jeans, sat down in the seat across the aisle.

I don't remember hippies being around town in 1966. Maybe he tried to get off here and the city fathers encouraged him to move on down the road. I'm not sure many places in Middle Falls would serve him looking like that in this era.

The long-haired man, who appeared to be in his early twenties, carried a guitar case, which he placed on the seat beside him. He looked across the aisle at Michael, gave him a nod, then settled back for a nap.

Wish I had a guitar, then everyone would avoid me, too. If he whips it out and starts playing "Tom Dooley," or "Blowin' In the Wind," I might have to take it and smash it over his head.

Directly in front of that man, a fortyish woman in a faded blue dress and a hat straight out of the 1950s sat down and arranged herself. She took out a bag of knitting and set to work, ignoring everyone around her.

Before they left the Middle Falls depot, the bus was almost half full. It was possible to drive from Middle Falls, Oregon, to Jenkins Grove in five hours. Because the bus would stop at every farmhouse, henhouse and outhouse, their projected drive time was instead eight and a half hours, with a thirty-minute layover in Coos Bay for lunch.

As he left the house, his father had told him that he could make himself a sandwich to take with him if he wanted, but he damn well wasn't paying for him to eat out on the trip. His mother, in a rare display of maternal love, slipped him two one-dollar bills as she gave him a brief hug and a distant air kiss on his way out the door.

Michael had inquired after Tess, but his father had smiled contentedly and said, "She took a half day today."

In other words, he didn't want to give me a chance to say goodbye to the one person in the house I care about. Bastard. Doesn't matter now, he's behind me. I wonder what's ahead?

Ninety minutes into the trip, the long-haired man rousted himself from his nap. He rubbed a hand across his straggly beard, then glanced at Michael with a wink. Michael rolled his eyes and stared out at the passing countryside.

The man leaned across the aisle and said, "Hey, buddy. I'm Glenn. What's your name?"

Michael continued to stare out the window several beats longer, so that Glenn would have no doubt about whether he was being ignored. Finally, he turned and said, "My name is, I don't like to be bothered by fruity hippies who smell like patchouli and marijuana."

Glenn flushed and turned away.

That ought to shut down conversation for the rest of the trip.

Glenn sat silent for several miles, then opened the guitar case. He fiddled with it, tuning it, playing a number of false starts, then began to sing softly. Michael had never heard the song before, but figured that it must have been called "*Plastic Jesus,*" based on how often that phrase was repeated throughout the song.

He started singing softly, but picked up a little volume as he got into the song, singing about "magnetized Mary" and how he was fine and dandy, as long as he had plastic Jesus sitting on the dashboard of his car.

Hey, could be worse. Could have been "Kumbaya."

The woman who sat in front of Glenn seemed oblivious to what he was doing, but after one verse, something about plastic Jesus being hollow and using him as a flask, she stiffened. She threw her knitting down and stood up a little too quickly. The shim and sway of the bus made her lose her footing, and she nearly ended up across the aisle, in the lap of a man dressed in overalls. She recovered, though, and took a threatening step toward Glenn, who played on, eyes closed, unaware of anything except for the next verse.

"Young man, that is my savior you are singing about!" Her eyes blazed and she quivered with righteous anger.

Glenn's eyes shot open in surprise. He stopped singing, but his hands kept playing the guitar. "Wh-what?" he said.

"Jesus Christ is my Lord and Savior. I will not sit quietly by and listen to him be defamed by you."

"Whoa, hold on, lady. That's not what this song is about. It's not sacrilegious. It just makes fun of people who try to act all high and mighty with Jesus when they ain't. That's all."

The woman shook her head in tight, tiny shakes. "No sir. *No* sir. That is not okay with me." Tears of anger welled in her eyes.

Glenn opened his mouth to speak, thought better of it, then brushed the hair out of his eyes. "Sorry, ma'am. I really didn't mean any offense. It's just a lark."

"There are many things to joke about. That's not one of them," she said, and turned and sat down with a huge exhalation.

Well. That oughta shut him up for a while.

The bus driver, a man in his sixties with gray hair and a gray uniform, called back over his shoulder, "Is there a problem? No music on the bus, please. It bothers the other riders. Thank you."

Glenn placed his guitar back in the case, set it beside him, and shuffled his hair into a veil over his eyes.

Aside from announcements about what stop was next, the rest of the trip was made in silence.

Chapter Eighteen

The Greyhound pulled into what passed for the Jenkins Cove bus station—a Shell gas station with all its lights turned off. The station sat alone on the side of Highway 101, with no other businesses in sight. Michael was the only passenger to get on or off. The driver clambered down after him, retrieved his suitcase from the bowels of the bus, and dropped it at his feet. Without a word, he climbed back on board and, with a hiss of air brakes releasing, turned back onto the highway. A few moments later, the bus was gone.

Michael looked around. The Shell station was locked up tight. The only sound was a battalion of frogs singing in chorus somewhere to his right. He took a Payday candy bar he had bought in Coos Bay out of his jacket pocket and unwrapped half of it.

Save the other half for breakfast, just in case I'm still sitting here.

The clock on the wall inside the station, in the shape of a seashell, glowed yellow. 9:20.

Michael pulled the collar of his jacket up over his neck. It wasn't cold yet, but once darkness settled in, he could see where it might be.

Worst-case scenario, I guess I can put all the clothes in my suitcase on to stay warm. I'll look like the Michelin Man, but who cares?

Down the road to Michael's left, a pair of headlights shone around a corner. As it drew nearer, Michael could see it was an olive drab Jeep. It pulled into the station without signaling and rolled to a stop in front of him. A teenage boy, all blond hair and angry acne, sat behind the wheel.

"C'mon, kid, there's no other vehicle dispatched to get you. Either get in or walk, and it's about five miles to the school."

Michael stood, grabbed his suitcase and put it in the back seat. The Jeep had no top, and no doors. It was a bit of a struggle, but Michael climbed up and in.

The teenager behind the wheel turned his head and looked Michael up and down. "Sit back and hold on."

He ground the gears and the Jeep leapt forward, leaving a spray of gravel behind them. The northern California air was a lot colder at 60 mph, so Michael zipped his jacket. His hair whipped straight up and his eyes watered a bit.

"Your dad a senator or something?" the boy shouted over the whipping wind.

That caught Michael off-guard. He shook his head.

"He must be something important."

"Why?"

"Academy's closed for the summer. Everyone has scattered to the four winds, but here I am, picking you up."

Michael chewed on that for a mile or so. *So this place is mostly empty? That might not be too bad, at least at first.*

Five minutes later, they pulled into a gated private road on the left. The gate was formidable—brick columns on each side, a ten-foot-high black gate with spikes on each bar—but it was open and they drove right in. They drove through the twilight, tall elm trees encroaching on both sides of the road.

Half a mile later, the trees parted and they entered a driveway that circled an immense lawn at least two acres in size. As they faced the largest building, the Jeep's headlights illuminated a gold and black sign: *Hartfield Military Academy, where boys become men and men become soldiers.*

The driver glanced over at Michael and saw him reading the sign. "That's our motto. Ready to become a man?" He laughed, drove around the driveway, and stopped in front of an impressive brick building three stories tall, with white columns supporting a pediment. It looked substantial enough to survive even the legendary California earthquakes, which is exactly what it had done for more than fifty years.

"C'mon," the teenager said, hopping nimbly out of the Jeep. "I'll show you where to put your stuff, then I am officially off duty for the night."

Michael got out, stood on tiptoe to retrieve his suitcase, and hauled it over the side of the Jeep. It wasn't very heavy, but it thumped down onto the gravel. Michael grabbed it again and chased after the retreating figure of his driver, who pointedly wasn't waiting for him.

The main doors were magnificent. Hand-carved designs in solid oak, nine feet tall. They led into an equally impressive foyer, which had high-backed chairs upholstered in red velvet scattered around the sides, each lit by a small pool of muted yellow light from a floor lamp. A chandelier that wouldn't have been out of place in a Las Vegas casino hung from the ceiling.

The driver turned to Michael. He was wearing an olive drab jumpsuit with a name over the breast pocket: Curt.

The guy who founded this place was Curtis. The guy who runs it is his grandson, Curtis. What are the odds that this guy is another one in line to run this place eventually? Pretty damn good.

"This is the great hall," Curt said, waving his hand expansively. "You won't spend any time in here. This is for guests—parents and military muckety-mucks—not cadets."

Cadet. Is that what I am now? I guess so.

"What's your name, again?"

"Hollister. Michael Hollister."

"If you're unlucky, you'll get a nickname. You won't like it. Nobody does. Until then, you are Cadet Hollister. Understand?"

Michael nodded.

"I'm Cadet Hartfield, or you can call me 'Sir' or 'Prefect.' Anything else will not be answered, and will result in punishment. Understood? Any questions?"

Michael knew it was best to keep a low profile, but he still said, "Sir. Did you get a nickname you didn't like, sir?" He did manage to keep any trace of a smile off his face.

Curt flushed, then turned and strode double-time across the great hall, toward a set of double doors in the back. Michael grabbed his suitcase and followed as fast as his legs would allow. Curt pushed through the double doors onto a sidewalk that led to a two-story building with a flat mansard roof. Red doors punctuated each end of the building, and Curt used the far door. Michael struggled to catch up, barely making it inside before the heavy door slammed shut.

Inside was a hallway running the entire length of the building, with only two doors on each side. Curtis walked to a door on the left and pushed it open. "This is home, at least until the prefect in charge of your unit gets back here next month and you are assigned your regular quarters. Enjoy the privacy, cadet. In the fall, you'll be sharing with a few dozen of your new closest friends."

The room was long, with another door at the back that Michael assumed led to a communal bathroom. On each side of the aisle down the middle of the room were eight steel-framed bunk beds. Two footlockers stood lengthwise at the end of each bunk.

"That's where your stuff goes," Curt said, pointing to a locker. If you've got more than will fit in there, you might as well toss it. You won't need it, anyway. When you've unpacked your suitcase, put it on top of the locker. It will be collected and stored until you go home for a visit."

Each bed had a thin mattress, rolled up, with a small pillow on top. "Pick whichever bunk you want for the summer. You'll be assigned your permanent home when the new semester starts. During the summer, meals are served one building over, in the staff dining room. Breakfast is at oh-six-hundred. If you get there one minute late, the doors will be locked and the next meal will be at 1200 hours. Being on time is very important at Hartfield Academy. You might as well learn that now."

Curt snap-turned, went out the door and closed it behind him.

Aside from the bunks and lockers, there was no other furniture in the room.

Spartan. What else would you expect from a place with a motto like "We turn boys into men and men into soldiers," or whatever nonsense was on the sign out front.

Michael pushed the door open and poked his head outside the room. Quiet as a tomb.

Must be all alone here. They really weren't expecting students this early. Must have cost dear old Father a pretty penny to get rid of me. Good.

Michael went to the door at the back and pushed it open. There was no locking mechanism.

Privacy is going to be in short supply once the semester starts.

Inside was a tile floor, half a dozen washbasins, toilets, and showers.

Michael crept out to the exterior door and pushed against it. It opened without a sound. *They're not locking me in, so at least I'm not a prisoner. Or, at least, not yet.*

Michael slipped off one of his Keds and wedged it into the door. Out in the cool night air, he took his other shoe and socks off and placed them against the building. Full darkness had descended, but a three-quarter moon gave light to see well enough. He stood to get his bearings, so he wouldn't get lost.

Great Hall there. Staff dining room probably over there. More buildings that look like barracks over there. Okay. He slipped between the shadows of the buildings, always waiting for a sentry to challenge him with a "Who goes there?" but none came.

I wonder if this place is fenced in. Let's find out.

He walked to the rear buildings: oversized, two-story wood structures that Michael assumed were the rest of the barracks. Behind them was another huge grass lawn, this one with a cinder track cut through it. Michael ventured onto the field but hurried as he did so. He felt exposed out in the open. He reached the far end of the mowed grass, which was bordered with more overgrown grass and weeds. He took five more steps forward and came to a halt. Two feet in front of him was a drop-off that led to another, and another. At the bottom of the cliffs lay large rocks, then a small thread of sandy beach and the Pacific Ocean. Moonlight glimmered over the chop of the waves.

Holy shit, what a view! Why in the hell would they use land like this for a crappy boys' school? They could develop this and sell this land for millions.

Michael stood looking out over the Pacific for a long time but eventually got cold and picked his way back to his room. He had a moment of panic when he thought he was lost, but he was just turned around. He found the door that still had his shoe wedged into it, picked up his other shoe and socks, and made his way back to what was, for the moment, his room.

Well. I guess this is it. Home. Might not be too bad, if I can find something to keep myself from dying of boredom. At least I'm away from him.

Michael set his suitcase on a bed at the very back of the room and opened it. He'd had no idea what was in his suitcase all day, as Tess had packed it for him the night before. He riffled through the clothes. Socks, underwear, T-shirts, and pants. One pair of pajamas, which he tossed on the bed. As he did, he saw the edge of a piece of paper poking out of the top pocket of the pajamas.

It was torn off the notepad Tess kept beside the refrigerator. In Tess's neat script were six words: *Michael. I'm sorry. I didn't know.*

Michael drew a deep breath. A lump formed in his throat that made it painful to swallow. Tears formed in his eyes, but he blinked them away.

No crying here. No signs of weakness. Boys who cry, boys who are homesick, boys who wet the bed, will get the worst of it. Not me.

Chapter Nineteen

Michael woke the next morning before the sun was up. He had no watch, and there was no clock in the room, but he remembered seeing one in the bathroom. He padded there barefoot, relieved himself, and noted that it was 5:25. The Payday candy bar of the night before was long since gone, and he didn't want to miss breakfast.

He returned to his room and got dressed in the same clothes he had worn the day before.

Don't know what the laundry situation is like here, but no sense in going through clothes when I don't need to.

Once dressed, he pushed out into the foggy coastal air. Summer, yes, but summer by the ocean, which left a slippery coating of dew on every surface.

Now. What the hell did "one building over" mean?

Michael walked to the building directly across from the one where he had slept, but it was a replica of the building he had stayed in, and it was locked tight. Kitty corner from that, he saw another building with a glassed-in entryway and standard-sized double doors. A simple sign above the doors read, "Staff Only."

Michael walked forward when he saw, through the glass, an older man emerging from an interior door. The man held up his hand in the universal "wait a minute" sign. He pulled a key ring from his belt, searched through dozens of keys for the right one, then unlocked the exterior door.

"You're early. Must be hungry."

"Curt said if I was late, I didn't eat."

"Curt's right, so, good for you for being early. Come in, you can help me set things out."

Through the interior doors he came into an open room with half a dozen round tables scattered about, each covered in a white plastic tablecloth.

"Follow me," the old man said. Michael did, noting that he walked with a slightly stooped gait and a pronounced limp. He pushed through a swinging door at the side of the room. When Michael followed, he saw metal platters loaded with sausage, scrambled eggs, and pancakes.

The smell filled his nostrils and made his knees weak.

"Those are heavy," the old man said, nodding to the platters of food. "I'll get them. You start carrying this stuff out." He waved toward pitchers of orange and apple juice, bottles of syrup and bowls of butter.

In the dining room, the old man said, "Put them down here. Skeleton crew in the summer, so we use one table to serve. Go on, get yourself a plate and dig in." He glanced at the clock, which read 5:55. "Everyone else will be here in the next two minutes."

Michael grabbed a plate off the stack and filled it. He moved to the farthest table, sat down and began to eat. Everything was delicious, but he found that he had overestimated the ability of his eight-year-old stomach to accommodate food. Halfway through the plate, he was stuffed to bursting.

At two minutes to six, the doors burst open and a small line of men walked through. They were all neatly dressed in uniforms with the Hartfield Academy logo on both shoulders, along with insignia that no doubt indicated some rank, had Michael known what each represented. Many of the men had catastrophic injuries—missing limbs, visible scars, terrible limps.

None of the men spoke; instead, they quietly moved to the long table with the food, loaded their plates and sat down at the same table.

The sound of silverware scratching against plates was the only sound as breakfast proceeded. The older man, whom Michael had decided to call "Cook" in his mind, sat with the other men and ate.

Michael did his best to persevere over the food he had mounded on his plate, but in the end, the physical limitations of his stomach did him in. He looked around, wondering where to put the remaining food on his plate, but didn't see anything obvious.

The oldest man sitting at the table stood, stacked his dishes and silverware back on the food table, then walked straight toward Michael. He was of average height and slightly on the lean side. What remained of his gray hair was in a crew cut. He looked down at the half-filled plate.

"My name is Peterson. You can call me sir, or Captain. At Hartfield, we eat all the food we take. This is your first meal here, so consider this your only warning. If you leave food on your plate again, it will be wrapped and served to you as your next meal. Understand?"

Michael nodded.

The man looked Michael up and down, from his slightly floppy haircut to his white T-shirt and khakis to his Keds. "We'll need to get you a haircut and uniform immediately. We never wear civilian clothes unless we are leaving the Academy for the day. You can provide your own socks and underwear, as long as it meets our standards."

So, my Batman underwear and argyle socks are a definite no-no, then?

Michael nodded again.

"Put your plate on the serving table, then follow me." He managed to make the word *plate* sound distasteful.

Michael hustled it to the table. All the other plates were empty. He set his off to the side of them and jogged to catch up with Captain Peterson, who turned down a side hall, then pushed into a small room marked *Supplies.*

He cast an appraising eye over Michael, then searched through several stacks of shirts and pants. He plucked out three khaki shirts, two pairs of navy blue pants, and two pairs of equally blue shorts, stacked them, and handed them to Michael. "What's your shoe size?"

"I don't know, sir."

"Cadet, you need to know that information. Take off your shoe."

Michael removed his shoe and handed it into Peterson's outstretched hand, who turned it over and peered at the bottom.

"Thirteen, eh? I'm not going to have anything that small until we get our new supplies in. Congratulations. You just got promoted to a size one." He plucked a pair of boots off a shelf and stacked them on top of the pile Michael was holding. He glanced at his watch. "I'll need you to report for work at oh-eight-hundred sharp, at the big flower bed at the front of the school."

"Work?"

"Yes, work, cadet. Everyone works at Hartfield. Did you have visions of floating around the Academy swimming pool by yourself all day while everyone else works? Be at the front flower beds by oh-eight-hundred. Wait, one more thing."

He opened a drawer behind him and withdrew a large electric hair trimmer. "Stand still."

Michael winced, but closed his eyes and stood as frozen as a doe in the headlights of an onrushing Camaro.

Ninety seconds later, all of Michael's hair was on the ground.

Michael rubbed his hand over his almost-nonexistent stubble.

Whatever. Who cares. Hair grows back.

Peterson admired his handiwork, then reached to the top of one of the shelving units and produced a blue cadet hat. "Here. You're going to be working outside, so you'll need this."

Michael didn't know if he was supposed to salute or not, so he settled for a nod. Before he was out the door, Peterson had a broom out and was sweeping up the hair.

Michael made his way back to his room.

Okay. It could be worse. Food's good. So far, no one's trying to sneak into my bunk in the middle of the night. I have to work, but there's worse things than that, I guess.

Michael felt tired and heavy-lidded after a late night and early morning, but he resisted lying down on his bunk for his free hour.

Not going to make a shitty impression by being late first thing.

Instead, he changed into the Academy uniform, choosing the shorts over the pants, and including the boots. He stared at himself in the mirror in the bathroom. He rubbed his hand again over the stubble that had been his hair a few minutes before. The boots seemed a bit too big, but the khaki shirt with the Hartfield emblem above the left breast pocket fit well. He put the blue cadet hat on and pushed it down into a slightly rakish angle.

Totally different. Shave all my hair off, put me in a uniform, and I look ... I don't know ... more adult, I guess. Since I actually am an adult, that's good, right?

Michael left the barracks and walked around the campus, mapping it in his mind, marking spots to explore later, under cover of darkness.

By 7:45, he was waiting in front of the flower bed that ringed the large grassy area at the front of the school. There was a towering flagpole dead center, with an American flag the size of Clayton Hollister's Cadillac flapping in the coastal breeze. Beside that was a slightly shorter pole with a Hollister Academy flag.

You know you've arrived when you go to a school that has its own flag.

Curtis M. Hartfield IV, his chauffeur of the previous night, approached from the west. Where Michael still felt stiff and uncomfortable in his newly issued uniform, Curt wore his like he had been born to it.

"Right on time, cadet. Good idea."

Michael squinted at him and said, "Fifteen minutes early, actually."

"Fifteen minutes early *is* right on time, cadet. Good that you've figured that out already. Now. This flower bed hasn't been weeded since school ended. It is a tragic tale of man vs. nature, with nature winning at the moment. You will spend your day here, reversing that outcome. Am I clear?"

"What tools do I have?"

"Tools? Cadet, you have those marvelous tools at the end of your arms. Eight fingers and two thumbs, which separate us from the apes."

Weird. Last night, he sounded almost like a normal teenager. Today, back on home turf, he sounds like a shrunken-down version of Peterson.

"Once you collect a big enough pile of weeds, there is a wheelbarrow in the gardening shed at the back of the compound. Weeds can be dumped in the burn pile beside the shed. Any questions?"

"How many kids are here right now?"

"Not the kind of question I was talking about, but I'll give you a freebie. There are three cadets on campus. Me, you, and my brother, Max. You'll meet Max at lunch. He skips breakfast, just like me, because it's not worth waking up that early to eat the same sausage, eggs, and pancakes every damn day."

Curt turned to leave, then stopped. When he turned back around, his official persona slipped away for a moment. He made steady eye contact with Michael.

"Max is ... slow. He's twelve, but he's the only cadet who has a separate room." Curt nodded his head in the direction of the big building. "He's slow, but he's not stupid. If I hear of you or anyone being mean to Max, they're gonna get whatever they dished out back in quadruple. Understand?"

Michael nodded, then said, "I don't have a watch. How will I know when it's time for lunch?"

Curt pointed to a bell tower atop the main building. "That bell rings exactly fifteen minutes before lunch and dinner. When you hear it, get washed up and report for chow."

Curt spun neatly and walked back the direction he had come.

Michael kneeled down and gave a test tug on the first weed of the day. It did not give way easily.

Chapter 20

Michael was grateful dinner was served early. The dinner bell pealed at 4:30. That meant the day was done. He had sent thousands of weeds to their final reward—enough to fill three wheelbarrow loads to overflowing. His back ached, the muscles in his arms quivered, and the back of his neck was red with sunburn, even though it had been overcast all afternoon.

He stood, brushed as much of the caked-on dirt off his knees as he could, and looked at what he had accomplished. A day's hard labor had weeded a quarter of the front flower bed.

Gonna be here for a few days, I guess.

Dinner, like breakfast and lunch, was consumed mostly in silence.

Have these guys all taken a vow of silence, or do they just have nothing to say? Either way, fine by me. I am dead to the world.

Peterson had come by the front flower beds to inspect his work in midafternoon and had told him what his work schedule would be: breakfast to dinner, Monday through Friday, with after-hours and weekends free for study or physical activity. There were no televisions anywhere on the Academy grounds—at least none where Michael could watch them. Maybe the Commander had a TV tucked away somewhere in his private quarters so he could watch *Rat Patrol,* or *Gomer Pyle, USMC,* but nothing for cadets.

The personnel present for dinner were essentially the same as for breakfast, with two additions: Curt and Max Hartfield. Curt was tall and lean. Max was a head shorter and stockier, with a round face, split by a wide grin.

Curt and Max were already seated at a table when Michael came in. There were large serving bowls of salad and mashed potatoes and a heated tray of Salisbury steak. After so many hours of hard work, Michael was starved, but he didn't want to run afoul of the rules again and be served a cold dollop of leftover mashed potatoes for breakfast tomorrow, so he took much smaller portions than he wanted.

He turned toward an empty table, but Max, whose voice carried through the quiet room, said, "Hey! Hey, new boy! Come on, come on. Sit over here with us."

Michael did not want to eat with Curt and Max, or with anyone, for that matter. However, he also did not want Max to continue speaking so loudly and drawing attention to him. He reluctantly turned toward their table and sat down.

God, I hope he doesn't want to talk all during dinner.

As soon as Michael sat down, though, Max seemed to be satisfied. He graced Michael with a beaming smile, then tucked into a large mound of mashed potatoes with bites of Salisbury steak mixed into it. Curt ignored the whole situation and ate in silence, staring at his food.

Michael cleaned his plate and contemplated a second helping of potatoes but decided against it. As everyone dispersed, Michael approached Max, who seemed to be far and away the friendliest person he had met at Hartfield.

"Excuse me. Can I ask you a question?"

"Sure," Max said. His voice came out of his mouth, but it sounded like it took a U-turn through his nose first. "What's your name? I'm Max. You can call me Max."

"I'm Michael. Can you tell me where the library is?"

Max smiled, an unconcerned smile that showed off too-small teeth. He reached down and put an arm around Michael's shoulders. Michael pulled back, repulsed at being touched, but Max did not notice.

"Come on, Michael. I know you are new here, so I will show you where the library is, and anything else you want to see. You tell me, and I'll show you, okay?"

Michael managed to free himself from the embrace, but nodded.

Max led him outside, past several of the barracks, and into another one-story brick building. The interior was mostly one large room, with every inch of wall covered in tall shelves filled with books.

"Nice library."

Max nodded emphatically. "Da says it's the best military strategy and reference library outside of Washington DC." He seemed to be repeating something he had memorized. "There's no one here in the summertime, so you can only read the books here; you can't take them to your room. It's open until ten o'clock, though. That's lights-out."

"Okay. Got it. Is it just military stuff? No science fiction or sports books?"

Max looked at him, mouth agape. "This is the best military strategy and reference library outside of Washington DC."

Michael got it, but he couldn't resist.

"So, no Archie Comics or Dr. Seuss?"

Max frowned. "Are you making fun of me?"

Michael did his best to put a smile on his face and waved his hands. "No, no. Just kidding around. Okay, thanks, Max. I'm really tired. I'm gonna go to my room now."

Max's frown melted away. "Okay, Michael. Night-night."

Fifteen minutes later, Michael fell face-first across his bed and was fast asleep. There would be no fact-finding missions on this night.

Chapter Twenty-One

The next few days were just like the first—breakfast, work, lunch, work, dinner, then exhaustion. Eventually, his muscles grew used to the physical labor, and by the sixth night, he had enough energy to explore the school again.

He had found an old flashlight that still worked in the tool shed at the back of the Academy. Between that, the moonlight, and his good, young eyes, he was able to cover a lot of ground. He kept returning to the cliffs, looking for a path that might lead down to the water. After an hour of poking and prodding the entire length, he was convinced there was no way down.

He stood with his back to the ocean, arms outstretched, envisioning the layout of the campus. *Essentially a square, with the driveway bisecting it at the top, the buildings in the middle, and these cliffs as the bottom of the square. Only one way in, one way out.*

He looked south. There was a forest of dense foliage, underbrush, sycamores and alders extending from the very edge of the cliffs. He pushed into the forest, but found it slow going. He was just about to give up when he stumbled across a game trail. He followed that along for fifty yards, until it dead-ended into a rock wall.

Jesus. It's like this place is walled on all sides.

He turned to leave when the beam of the flashlight crisscrossed some vines hanging down the sheer wall, stirring a memory. He took a few steps forward and tentatively poked the vines.

The way they hang and move in the wind. There's something so familiar about that.

He used the flashlight to push some of the vines to the side. It was the mouth of a cave.

His legs nearly gave way.

A cave. A fucking cave.

His mind flew to another cave. Another lifetime. Images of himself, kneeling down in the dirt and dark, doing terrible things. Tiny skulls, arranged neatly on a natural shelf in the cave. He broke out in a cold sweat, even though the night air was cool and a stiff breeze rustled the leaves and brush around him. He twisted his head from side to side, cracking his neck.

No. No, this is a different life. I am different. I am not that person any more.

He swept the hanging vines away and explored the mouth of the cave with the flashlight.

Not that big. Maybe fifteen feet deep. Looks tall enough to stand up in, though. Terrible smell, too. Something's using this cave from time to time.

He swept the beam across the uneven floor and saw scattered piles of small bones and fur.

Gonna have to come back here in the daylight and check it out.

Michael stepped back and forced himself to focus his eyes. He made a mental note of where he was and how he had gotten there, then followed the trail back to the open air. He was relieved when he crawled into his bunk.

Chapter Twenty-Two

The hours turned to days, the days to weeks, as they always do. Michael spent his days pulling more weeds, polishing staircase railings, vacuuming the huge rooms, and doing whatever else Peterson could think of for him to do.

He spent evenings in the library. There really was no fiction there, but military nonfiction didn't have to be dry or boring. *The Art of War* by Sun Tzu may have been published 1,500 years earlier, but the accompanying text, which gave examples of each truism in the book, plucked from conflicts ranging from the Revolutionary War to a recent battle in Vietnam, brought the book to life. *Helmet for My Pillow,* by Robert Leckie, *Run Silent, Run Deep,* by Edward L. Beach, *The Guns of August,* by Barbara Tuchman, and *The Rommel Papers,* written by Erwin Rommel himself, all turned out to be fascinating reading for Michael. Every day, the stack of books he still wanted to read grew.

Several weeks after first arriving, Michael was back in the front flower beds, waging war against the treacherous weeds that would not accept defeat, when Curt rolled up with Max in the same Jeep he had used to pick him up the first night.

"Iggy's sending me into town to pick up supplies. Want to come?" "Iggy" was Peter Ignovich, whom Michael had once thought of as "Cook."

Michael stood, adjusted a crick in his back, and said, "Captain Peterson's got me on weed patrol."

Curt lowered his head and looked at Michael over the top of his sunglasses. "We'll only be gone a couple of hours. The weeds will still be there when we get back. C'mon."

Michael realized he hadn't been off the grounds of Hartfield since he had arrived. He nodded and had started to climb up and into the back seat when Max turned and yelled "Shotgun!" from the front passenger seat.

Curt laughed. "No need to call it when you're already riding it, Max."

"Right, right," Max said, memorizing another important rule to get him through life.

Curt turned right out of the academy's long driveway and headed down the coast toward Crescent City.

"So, where's Jenkin's Cove actually at?" Michael shouted at the front seat.

"Do you remember the gas station I picked you up at?" Curt met Michael's eyes in the rearview mirror.

Michael nodded.

"That was it. There was some hope that more businesses might spring up around it to service the Academy, but that never really happened. It's just a name that stuck."

"So where are we going?"

"Grayson's Mercantile in Crescent City. It's not far."

Half an hour later, they pulled into Crescent City, which wasn't a metropolis either, with a population barely over 3,000. Still, it was busy enough to have a few stoplights and a downtown business district.

Curt drove past a large store with a Grayson's Mercantile sign out front, turned right at the next block, and another down an alley behind the row of businesses. He stopped the Jeep and backed it neatly into a loading area.

"We're not picking up that much stuff. But the rules are, we pick up at the loading dock."

The three boys got out of the Jeep. Tall, acne-cursed Curt, short, moon-faced Max, and the even smaller Michael, all dressed in identical Hartfield uniforms.

The loading dock was empty, so they walked up the ramp, empty except for a large green industrial machine in one corner.

"You stay here and make sure no one messes with the Jeep, okay?"

Sure. What am I gonna do if someone does mess with it? Kick 'em in the kneecap?

Michael sat down on the edge of the loading dock and dangled his feet against the concrete. He wasn't interested in going into the store, anyway. He had no money, and there was nothing he needed.

Curt and Max disappeared inside for a stretch, then reappeared pushing a low, flat cart with half a dozen boxes stacked on it. Behind them were a boy and a girl wearing long red aprons with *Grayson's* in script across the front. They both looked to be Curt's age. The boy was a few inches shorter, but might have had Curt by fifteen pounds. The girl had shoulder-length brown hair and a pretty face.

Michael saw *something* pass between the girl and Curt—an unidentifiable look—but it flickered away.

The boy carried a stack of broken-down cardboard boxes over to the large metal machine and tossed them in. He shut the lid and pushed a button, and the machine went to work with much fury and noise. Thirty seconds later, the boy opened the lid. The cardboard had been compressed.

Meanwhile, Curt, Max, and Michael each picked up a box and began loading the Jeep.

Looks like we've got just enough room for this stuff and, maybe, me. I might have to ride home on top of a case of creamed corn or spinach, though.

The three of them were walking back up to get the last boxes when the boy in the red apron laughed loudly—a mean laugh, full of menace. Under his apron, he wore a white T-shirt with the left sleeve rolled up with a pack of cigarettes. He shook one out and laughed again, looking at Max.

Curt flushed but didn't say anything. Michael slowed down, then stopped, halfway up the ramp.

The boy lit his cigarette and flicked his ash toward Max. The girl snickered.

Under her breath, she sang, "Retard boy, you're my little retard boy," to the tune of "Soldier Boy" by The Shirelles.

Red apron boy laughed again, hawked, and spit a loogie toward Max.

Curt stepped between the boy and Max and said, "You're a real asshole, George. Just knock it off, will you? We'll be out of here in two minutes."

"Gotta go back and train to go kill some gooks?" He mimed using a submachine gun, complete with sound effects.

It was the girl's turn to laugh. "You kill me, Georgie. C'mon, let's go back to work." She pointedly put her arm through George's.

George nodded, then flicked his lit cigarette toward Max. It hit him just under his chin and fell down into his uniform shirt.

"Ow, ow, ow!" Max cried. "It's burning me! Curtis, it's burning me!"

Michael leaped toward Max, pulled his shirt out of his pants, and shook it until the cigarette fell out.

"It's okay, Max," Michael said. "I've got it. It's okay."

Curt turned and swung on George, but George knew it was coming. He easily ducked out of the way. He followed up with a roundhouse of his own that caught Curt flush on the nose. Blood spattered and Curt stumbled back, blinded.

George was off-balance from throwing the haymaker and Michael was already moving. He threw himself across the much bigger boy's knees in a full body block. George teetered on the edge of the loading dock, then pitched over backwards.

He hit the pavement beside the Jeep butt-first, but his head slammed into the concrete with a sickening thud.

For a moment, everyone stared down at the fallen boy.

Oh, shit. Didn't think that would actually work.

After a few seconds of quiet, George rolled over onto his side, revealing a red blotch on the pavement where his head had been. The girl screamed, a sound so piercing that Michel was sorry he had ears.

Curt, one hand over his nose, ran to Michael to help him up. He collected Max, who was crying, and hustled them both down the ramp and into the Jeep. He jumped into the driver's seat, threw the Jeep in gear, and sped away.

As they roared down the alley, Max yelled "Shotgun!" from the front seat.

Chapter Twenty-Three

Carrie had learned a few things. It didn't matter whether she opened her training manual at the beginning, middle, or end; she saw exactly the message she was supposed to. Also, when it came to a battle of patience and wills between her and the manual, the manual always won.

More practically, she had learned that she would have a lot of freedom in her job. She didn't have to do anything other than observe her charges if she didn't want to. She didn't have to do mean things to them just to get a reaction. Also, she had no say about whom she watched over. No matter what Bertellia said, it kind of *was* like watching television; it was just watching real life instead of something scripted.

She hadn't gotten anything but fortune-cookie answers—*If you seek light, turn your gaze inward*—in what felt like eons, though. She blew a gust of air up at her bangs. All around her, others were dutifully turning pages, working, working.

I must be the only idiot in the group that can't figure out how to work this thing properly.

She rolled her neck, loosened her shoulders, took a deep breath and held it.

I can't do it. I give up.

The book became a pyxis.

You have got to be kidding me.

Bertellia appeared at her side. "Congratulations, you have finished your training."

All around her, the others raised their eyes and stared at her. Carrie could read their thoughts: *What makes her so special?*

I have no clue.

"How in the world can you say I've finished? I couldn't make it tell me anything. Finally, I gave up."

"You have answered your own question, and you are correct. You couldn't make it tell you anything. It sometimes takes novitiates millennia to learn that. You managed it in a surpassingly short time." Bertellia fixed Carrie with a thoughtful look. "The true key is that you gave up."

"Giving up is a *good* thing?"

"Of course. There are times it is the only path to the next level. We must admit how much we do not know before we can learn the things we need. Come, now."

Carrie had thought the room she was in was immense. Now, she was suddenly in a structure that made that one feel like a broom closet. If there hadn't been a ceiling, she would have sworn she was in a vast outdoor world. There were two rows of desks that stretched as far as she could see.

"This is your desk. It is time for you to work. To feed the Machine."

Carrie sat at her new workspace. The pyxis turned slowly in a clockwise motion. A picture began to form.

"This will be your first charge. You will be able to learn anything you want to know about who they are. The pyxis will do the work of collecting for you. You will start with just one. Others will be added over time, as you become expert at your job."

Bertellia bent closer to the picture, which glowed a golden white at the edges. "Oh, my, look at all that emotion. That's a promising beginning for you."

Carrie focused on the picture, which showed a young boy, riding in the back of a Jeep.

Chapter Twenty-Four

No one talked on the way to the Academy. The combination of the roar of the Jeep's engine and the whistling wind made an involved conversation impossible. Curt dabbed gingerly at his nose with a handkerchief, Max hummed the tune to "Soldier Boy" over and over, and Michael thought furiously.

Have I screwed myself already? Shit. That kid's head was bleeding. If I killed him, what happens then? I don't love being here, working as a free labor force all day every day, but there are a lot worse places I could end up. If I get kicked out of Hartfield, then what will Father come up with to torment me?

Curt slowed to a stop at the same spot he had picked Michael up. "Jump out here, let me look you over."

Michael did as he was ordered. Curtis examined him. A small scuff on the knee of his pants; his uniform shirt was untucked. But Michael wasn't much worse for wear.

"You look okay. Good. Just go back to what you were doing here. Report for supper when the bell rings. I'll do my best to keep you out of this. And, Michael? Thanks."

It was the first time Curt had ever called him anything other than "Cadet" or "Hollister."

Michael knelt down in the flower bed and started pulling weeds again, but dread weighed heavily on him.

An hour later, the bell rang and Michael dusted himself off and headed for the latrine to wash up for dinner. He was intercepted by Captain Peterson.

"Did you go into town today with Curtis and Maxwell Hartfield?"

Michael looked at the ground for several seconds. *I'd like to say "no," but if he's asking the question, he already knows the answer.*

"Yes sir."

Peterson nodded. "Come with me. Commander Hartfield wants to see you."

Michael had been at the Academy almost a month, but aside from a few glimpses across a yard of a retreating back, he had never actually seen Curtis Hartfield III. These were not the circumstances he would have wanted for a first meeting.

Peterson led Michael into the great hall of the main building, down a heavily carpeted hallway and into a waiting room. There was a desk and a row of uncomfortable-looking chairs against the wall.

Peterson nodded toward the chairs. "Sit there." He knocked lightly, once, on the door to the inner office, paused for a moment, then let himself in, closing the door behind him.

Michael climbed up into one of the chairs, feet dangling, and waited. And waited. A small wall clock chimed five o'clock, which meant he had missed dinner.

Fine. Who cares? Don't think I could eat anything anyway, and I'd end up having leftover goulash or whatever we're having tonight for breakfast tomorrow.

Finally, the door opened quietly and Peterson took a half-step out, motioning for Michael to come inside.

Commander Hartfield's office was impressive. The window to his left looked out onto the front lawn, where Michael had been weeding a few minutes before. *Didn't know he could see me out there busting my butt.*

There were glass-fronted bookshelves along the wall behind him. Two flags hung down from poles in opposite corners: the American flag to his right, and the gold and blue Hartfield Academy flag to the left. His desk was massive, and Michael thought Hartfield was either a very tall man, or his chair was higher than anything else in the room. In front of the oak desk were three chairs. Two were already filled by Curt and Max Hartfield. Max appeared unconcerned. He waved and smiled at Michael. Curt stared straight ahead.

Curtis Hartfield III stood, and Michael realized he was indeed a tall man. Whereas his elder son was whippet-lean, Hartfield was solid and imposing. His craggy face was inscrutable. A full head of iron-gray hair came to a widow's peak in front.

"Cadet Hollister? Take a seat." His voice was gravel.

Michael did as he was told.

"You were at Grayson's Mercantile with my sons today."

It was not a question, so Michael sat still, unblinking.

"There was …" he paused to knock a pipe against an ashtray, "a conflict there. A boy, George Bittle, is hurt and in the hospital. Curtis says you were there, but only as a witness. The girl who was there," he referred to a piece of paper in front of him, "Lisa Wheeler, says you were actually the one who pushed this George off the dock."

He leaned forward a few inches. "Both can't be true. So, which is it?"

Michael glanced to his right, looking for some clue from Curt what to do.

"Look at me, son, don't look at him. You need to tell me the truth of what happened."

Shit. Shit, shit, shit. I'm screwed either way here, I think. I tell the truth, and Curt thinks I betrayed him. I lie, the truth comes out eventually, and I probably get kicked out.

"Curt said I was only a witness, sir, because he is trying to protect me. The boy who is injured threw a cigarette at Max, then suckerpunched Curt. I saw he was off-balance, so I did what I could. I pushed him down. I didn't intend for him to fall off the loading dock."

Well, that's most of the truth.

Hartfield leaned back in his chair. He allowed himself a small smile.

"That is an intelligent answer, Cadet. I forget. Why are you here with us in summer?"

Bullshit, you forgot. I don't think you forgot what you had for lunch fifteen years ago.

"I wasn't privy to the full scope of the discussion, sir. I believe my father just wanted me out of the house and kept pulling strings until he made that happen."

Hartfield chortled, a deep, bullfrog croak that ended as quickly as it began.

"I think you are one to keep an eye on, cadet. All right, enough nonsense. Curtis."

Curt sat even straighter, which Michael would have bet was impossible. "Sir."

"You had to choose from a conflicting set of orders here: to never cause problems in town, but to always protect your brother. I appreciate that you chose to protect your brother, but it was a bad decision. This girl being involved might have been as much on your mind as the cigarette thrown at Max. You can't afford to make bad decisions in the heat of battle. If you do, eventually, men will die, and it will be my fault, because I didn't train you properly. You are confined to campus for the rest of the summer and on MRE rations until school starts. I will deal with the local police on this matter."

He looked sharply at Captain Peterson, who had melted back into a wall. "I'm sure this George and Lisa both have some things on their records that will undermine their credibility. Have Morton do his normal research and dig up whatever he needs to take care of it."

"Yes, sir," Peterson said, making a notation on a clipboard.

"Hollister. It appears to me that you made the best decisions you could in a difficult situation. Impressive for one so young." He glanced at his watch. "I see I've made you miss dinner. No call for that. Please go to the canteen. I'll call Iggy and tell him to unlock the door and make you a plate."

Michael knew he was dismissed. He clambered down from the chair and opened the heavy door to the waiting room. He glanced back to see if he could catch Curt's eye, but he was still staring straight ahead.

Did I goof up?

Chapter Twenty-Five

Michael walked out of the office that evening sweating bullets about how Curt might react to him, but he needn't have worried. For the next few weeks, he never even saw him, and soon after, the school year started.

Cadets began to arrive early on the Sunday of Labor Day weekend. All across America, families were enjoying one last blowout barbecue or a day at the lake. Not so, the families of boys who would become men at Hartfield Academy. Those families drove from wherever they were to mark the start of a new year.

A few cars trickled in that morning, eager to disgorge their offspring and be on about their lives. By early afternoon, the cars became a steady stream of Buicks, Cadillacs, Fords, and Chevys. Not a single Datsun, Peugot, or Mercedes in sight. At two o'clock, it was difficult to find a parking spot along the great lawn, but by early evening, the boys, already dressed in their Hartfield Academy uniforms, were settling into their new quarters.

There were three barracks for the cadets and another for the staff. Each cadet barrack consisted of three floors, with one year per floor. The First Year, or third grade, barrack was the largest, because so many started at that age, but almost half had dropped out for one reason or another by the time they reached the upper years.

The other First Years look so small and scared, like they'd much rather crawl back into their parents' backseat and head for home. Of course, I'm sure people thought that about me, too, and life here is better than it was at home. So far. This place has been okay while it was empty. Add a few hundred boys ranging in age from eight to eighteen, though, and that might change. There will be bullies here, looking for victims. The logical place to look will be in the First Years.

A series of bleachers had been set up on the front lawn, and a welcome and orientation was held for both students and parents who weren't already on the road home to Portland, San Francisco, and points beyond.

The staff sat in folding chairs behind a lectern, and many of them came up to say a few words and make a point about the various rules of Hartfield Academy.

It all boils down to this: if you can think of it, they've already got a rule. If it's fun, you can't do it. If it's a lot of hard work, it's required. Oh, and be respectful of everyone above you, in age, rank, or both. Pretty simple.

Back in the First Year barrack, Michael found he had been assigned to the same bunk he had slept in all summer—bottom bunk, right side, all the way to the back, near the bathroom. The boy assigned to the bunk above him was a dark-haired, dark-eyed boy. He didn't speak to Michael or anyone as he unpacked his suitcase into his footlocker, set it on top as instructed, then climbed up and sat on his bunk, quietly watching the other boys with an amused expression on his face.

Now that there are so many people in here, you'd think they'd give us locks for our footlockers. No such luck, though. That means no real privacy, no way to stash anything anywhere.

The door to the barrack slammed open and a stocky older boy burst in, carrying a clipboard and a green duffel bag. "Hello, shit for brains. I am a Ninth Year. I have been assigned as your prefect. I will oversee you for the rest of the year. My name is Lt. Tim Pusser."

A few snickers sounded around the barracks.

Pusser homed in on them with long-practiced radar, walking up and down the aisle, making check marks on a piece of paper on his clipboard. He smiled, but it was a jack-o'-lantern grin. He nodded as though he understood. "Pusser's a funny name, isn't it? Lends itself to funny nicknames, doesn't it?" He pointed to a redheaded boy halfway down the left side. "You." He consulted his clipboard again. "Cadet Markson, is that right?"

The redheaded boy nodded, uncertainly.

"I saw you laugh. So, let's hear it. What's a funny nickname that Pusser makes you think of?"

Markson, still unpacking his suitcase, turned sunburn red, looked at the floor, and remained silent.

"Nothing? Damn. I was sure you were going to be the class clown. I am disappointed. Give me twenty-five push-ups."

The boy hesitated. Pusser took three long strides toward him and slammed his clipboard against the side of the bunk with a bang. "Now, cadet!"

Markson dropped down and started doing something that looked similar to push-ups.

"Oh my God!" Pusser yelled. "You look like a monkey humping a football, boy! Didn't anyone ever teach you how to do a proper push-up?"

Markson continued to pump his body up and down, butt pointed to the ceiling. He shook his head.

Pusser set his clipboard on the top bunk and dropped easily to the ground. He did one smooth push-up, then another, and another. He stood up without wrinkling his uniform. He had not broken a sweat. "You see that, cadet? That's how you do a push-up."

Markson nodded, but continued to struggle awkwardly.

"Stop, stop, just stop! You're embarrassing yourself, and since I am in command of this class, you are embarrassing me. I can see we'll all need a good round of callisthenics technique before lights-out tonight." He retrieved his clipboard and started to pace up and down the aisle between the bunks. "Where was I? Oh, right. My name is Lt. Tim Pusser." He paused, looked around. No one moved or snickered. In truth, no one breathed.

This guy's seen too many war movies, I think. What an idiot.

"I will be the officer in charge of your lives for the rest of your first year here at Hartfield Academy. After that, I will be gone, and a new officer will be in charge of making your life hell next year. In addition to the Academy's rules, I have a few of my own. Once it is lights-out, we will have total silence in this barrack. Feel a need to cry because you miss your mommy? Do it into a pillow so I don't hear it."

He got to the end of the row of bunks, turned, and looked at Michael briefly. Michael met his eyes and would not look away.

"If you need to use the bathroom in the middle of the night, do it, but do it quietly." He pointed one finger at his own face. "As you can see, I need all the beauty sleep I can get. If you wake me up, I will make sure everyone is awake, and we will drill for an hour, right here at our bunks."

He paused, surveyed his charges, and obviously found them wanting. "You want to make it here at Hartfield? Three things: Show up, keep up, and shut up."

Pusser retrieved his duffel bag, walked to the bunk at the front corner of the room, nearest the door. "This is my bunk. Yes, princesses, don't worry, I won't leave you alone. I will be right here with you all night, every night."

He looked at his watch. "It is twenty-one hundred hours. That gives you thirty minutes until lights out. Get your kits unpacked, then place your suitcases on top of your footlocker. Reveille is at oh-six-hundred."

Michael looked around at the other boys. Most of them were stripping down to T-shirts and underwear. No pajamas. Michael did the same, slipped under the green blanket, and closed his eyes.

I liked this place a lot better when I was the only one here. He looked around at the other boys. Most looked shell-shocked, but a few were already regaining an eight-year-old's false sense of invulnerability. *What would I have been like if I was that young? I'd have been just as scared as they are.*

Michael lay awake on his bunk, getting used to the reality of having so many bodies so close to him. Within fifteen minutes, a harsh noise started at the other end of the barrack.

Shit. That'll get Pusser all riled up.

It continued unabated, with an odd, resonant rhythm. Finally, curiosity got the better of him and Michael slipped out of his bunk on cat's feet. He took a few steps, then paused to see if he had been noticed. As he passed the bunks, several boys sat up and looked a question at him. He ignored them.

When he finally reached the far end, he discovered why Pusser hadn't yelled at the transgressor.

He *was* the transgressor. He was lying flat on his back, head back, mouth wide open, with a steady chainsaw noise emanating from his larynx. Michael stifled a laugh, then walked much more deliberately back to his bunk.

It took Michael hours to go to sleep, but he wasn't alone. Deep into the night, he heard muffled sighs and crying.

Chapter Twenty-Six

Each class at Hartfield is given a mascot. The First Years of 1966 were dubbed "The Turtles" by Lieutenant Pusser. He said it was because they were so small, and most baby sea turtles got eaten by carnivores as they made their first dash to the ocean. Insulting or not, it was their nickname, and it would stay with the class until graduation.

The life of a Turtle at Hartfield Academy was hard, but aside from nightly tirades from Pusser, it was good enough. Reveille played through speakers at both ends of the barracks at 6 a.m. sharp, Monday through Friday. On weekends, they were allowed to sleep in until 6:30. They didn't have class on weekends, but Pusser drilled them endlessly around the track, teaching formation, discipline and stamina. Pusser was not a smart boy, but he could march. Soon enough, so could all the Turtles.

Another of Pusser's special rules was that every boy's feet had to be on the floor within thirty seconds of reveille. On the second day, several boys dawdled a bit and found themselves dumped on the cold concrete floor by Pusser. He was surprisingly quick first thing in the morning, especially when hunting layabouts. By the fifth day, each boy had learned to put his feet on the floor while still mostly asleep, often not truly waking up until he was completely dressed.

All Turtles were to be lined up in front of their bunks by 6:25. Breakfast was served in the huge cafeteria at 6:30. On the way to breakfast that first day, Pusser said, "Meals at Hartfield are for nutrition, not for socializing and not for grab-assing. Eat everything you take, stack your plate, and be ready for class by oh-seven-hundred."

Classes were fifty-five minutes long and started on the hour, for seven hours each day. There were no optional classes.

The first class of the first day was English, taught by Mr. Guzman, a black-haired man with a scarred face and the left arm of his uniform neatly folded and safety-pinned just below his shoulder.

Unlike Middle Falls Elementary, where Michael had stayed in the same room all day, Hartfield Academy ran more like a high school, with boys moving from class to class, teacher to teacher, each hour.

"Good morning," Mr. Guzman said, leaning back against his desk. "We will start by saying the Pledge of Allegiance." All twenty-four boys rose as one, faced the flag in the front corner of the room, and saluted. They recited, "I pledge allegiance to the flag of the United States of America, and to the Republic for which it stands, one nation under God, indivisible, with liberty and justice for all."

"Good," Guzman said. "I'm glad that we all know the Pledge. Later on this year, we'll talk more about it, and what it really means for each of us. For now, though, it's enough that you all know it. Now, who likes to read?"

No hands went up.

"We'll have to see if we can do something about that. You there," he said, pointing to a boy in the front row. "What's your name?"

"Jenkins, sir."

"Very good. Cadet Jenkins, please pass the books out that are here on my desk." He pointed to several dozen paperback books.

"This book is called *The Island of the Blue Dolphins*. We have ..." he glanced over his shoulder at the clock on the wall, "Fifty minutes left in class. Let's take 40 minutes to read the first two chapters, then we'll discuss them."

So, what do I do? Act like I'm a typical eight-year-old again and die of boredom for the next however many years, or show them what I really know, and get treated like a freak?

The book Michael received was soft with wear, but there were no rips or tears on the cover or pages. He read quickly through the first two chapters, then looked at the clock on the wall. There were still forty minutes left in class. The other boys were still on the first two pages, lips moving as they read silently, or tracing along each line with a finger. Michael closed the book, folded his hands, and looked straight ahead.

A moment later, Mr. Guzman stood over Michael. "Cadet Hollister. Am I to assume that you have already finished your reading?"

Heads popped up to look at Michael all over the class. One boy whispered, "No way," under his breath.

"Yes, sir," Michael said.

"Can you tell me what the first two chapters are about?"

"They're about a young girl and her tribe living on an island. Some Russians come and bargain with them to hunt the otters. They negotiate and come to an agreement. In the second chapter, the tribe finds a bunch of fish and eat it all themselves. The Russians ask them to share the fish, but the tribe doesn't want to share. I would guess that doesn't turn out very well for the tribe."

"Good, good. And, have you read this book before?"

"No."

"I see. You're a fast reader, then. I will come up with some special assignments for you. In the meantime, why don't you just read ahead."

Michael nodded and returned to the book, but noticed that several of the other boys were looking at him out of the corner of their eyes.

The next class was general math, taught by Mr. Bennett. He handed out a large sheaf of basic math problems.

"Cadets, work your way through these problems as quickly as you can. Accuracy counts, of course, but I need to see if you are having trouble in any particular areas."

Michael riffled through the problems. Addition. Subtraction. Multiplication and some long division. He sighed and went to work.

Five minutes later, he handed the completed work in and returned to his desk.

Mr. Bennett glanced through the problems, then hooked a finger at Michael. When Michael arrived back at his desk, he said, "Good work, cadet. Do you have something with you to read?"

Michael nodded and went back to his desk. He pulled out *The Island of the Blue Dolphin*.

By the end of the period, he was almost finished with it. More boys stared at him.

Michael kept it up through each period, acing tests in social studies, geography, and science.

Might as well see what they do with me if they know what I am. Or, at least, partially know what I am. Not sure what *they'd do if they really knew what I was.*

Chapter Twenty-Seven

"You've got to be kidding me. Michael Hollister? That child is really Michael Hollister?"

Carrie was speaking out loud, but to no one in particular. Arbann, who sat at the desk next to hers, never moved her eyes from what she was doing.

Carrie took a deep breath and held it. "Bertellia," she said, with as much calm as she could muster, "can you hear me?"

Of course I can hear you," Bertellia's disembodied voice said. "I can always hear you. You just weren't saying anything that needed an answer."

"He killed me. Do you understand? He wrapped his slimy hands around my throat and choked me to death. My last memory on Earth is of his face, leering at me."

"Yes. So?"

"So? Come on. Even you guys aren't that clueless, are you? I'm not going to spend my time now, watching him do ... whatever it is he's going to do, to whoever he will do it to next."

"That's fine. You don't have to."

Carrie sat back a bit. She didn't know where to look, since she was talking to someone who wasn't anywhere in sight. Her voice lowered. "Okay. That's better. So, what do I have to do to get him off my pyxis?"

"Oh, you can't." Bertellia's voice showed a small amount of surprise.

Carrie shook her head. "I just told you, I won't spend my time watching the life of the horrible person who killed me."

"And I told you that you don't have to. So. What would you like to do instead? The filing room? Recycle to Earth?"

Carrie's smile was tinged with bitterness. "I see how it is."

"He did you a favor, you know."

"Oh, come on."

"You were stuck, repeating the same cycle over and over. Now you're not. He's part of your true family. True families are rarely born together on Earth."

A shudder started at the base of Carrie's spine and carried up to the top of her head.

"That figures. The person I hate most is part of some weird cosmic family."

"You are doing so well, Carrie. You figure things out much more quickly than most."

"You must be part of my family, too, because there are times I really hate you, too."

"Of course you do. I have to feed the Machine as well."

Bertellia was gone.

Well that's great. Carrie was staring intently at her pyxis. She spent time watching Michael perform so well on test after test.

Of course he's doing well. He's a nineteen-year-old man taking tests designed for eight-year-olds. Ooof.

She perked up a bit when she saw him change into shorts and a T-shirt. She hadn't known a lot about Michael in her first life, but she did remember how badly he got embarrassed in a dodgeball game.

He is not athletic. Let's see how being older helps him here.

She watched as a class of boys lined up on a track to run. Just as they began the run, Carrie's hand reached out and gave the pyxis a tiny shake.

"Oh!" she exclaimed. "Oh my."

Chapter Twenty-Eight

Michael's run of brilliance came to a halt in the sixth hour: PE. Michael had never been athletic, and reincarnating his nineteen-year-old mind inside an eight-year-old body had not made him any more so.

Mr. Lawson, the PE teacher, began by lining them up at the start/finish line of the quarter-mile track at the back of the Academy. "One lap around, cadets, as fast as you can go." He blew one shrill blast on his whistle, and the boys took off. A few of the more coordinated boys jumped out ahead of the pack. The remainder looked remarkably like their turtle namesake.

At the very rear of that pack was Michael Hollister. He stumbled badly at the beginning, fell to his knees after tripping over nothing in particular, then struggled across the finish line behind everyone but Freddy Cashmore, who was asthmatic and slightly pigeon-toed. Dominick Davidner, his dark-haired bunk-mate, had been the first across the finish line. When Michael finally crossed, Dominick stood beside him and whispered, "Well, that's a relief. I thought you were perfect at everything, but I guess not."

Michael shot him a look, but Dominick was smiling and slapped Michael on the back before jogging off to their next exercise. He didn't notice that Michael had flinched away from him.

The rest of the PE class followed the pattern, no matter what the exercise—leg lifts, wind sprints, jumping jacks, or deep squats. If Michael wasn't the worst boy in class, he was in the bottom two.

I hate this shit. What's next, dodgeball?

111

Chapter Twenty-Nine

The next day, as soon as Mr. Guzman called class to order, he said, "Cadet Hollister, you are wanted in the main building by Commander Hartfield. Report there at once, and take your books with you."

A quiet "Ooooohhh" rippled through the class.

Michael flushed slightly but gathered his books and headed across campus to the main building. He hadn't been inside since the day he, Curt, and Max had been interrogated by Hartfield. In fact, he hadn't seen much of Curt since then, although he had still eaten most meals with Max during the summer.

Michael opened the door that led into Commander Hartfield's outer office. Captain Peterson was seated at the outside desk, talking on the telephone. He pointed Michael to the chairs against the wall. A few minutes later, he hung up the phone and looked Michael over as though seeing him for the first time. He stood, opened the door to the inner office, and said, "Come in, cadet."

The office was unchanged from when he had seen it a month before. Even Commander Hartfield looked the same—as though he didn't sleep, or eat, or go to the movies, but simply sat behind that desk, dealing with the business of turning young boys into men and men into soldiers twenty-four hours a day.

"Sit down, cadet," Peterson said.

Michael sat in the same chair he had been in a month earlier.

Commander Hartfield had a file open on his desk and was studying it. He turned a page, read for a moment, then turned another. Finally, he looked across at Michael.

He tapped a meaty finger against the file in front of him. "These are your records from Middle Falls Elementary. The boy I see reflected in these grades and test results is not the same boy who whipped through our first-day tests. How do you explain the discrepancy?"

It's easy. I lived another decade past those test results, killed someone, got caught, killed myself, and woke up back in this shitty little body. Is that so hard for you to understand?

Michael shrugged, but remained mute.

"There's nothing wrong with your marks, of course, or your test results. You wouldn't be sitting here if there were, no matter how many strings your father pulled. But, there's also nothing extraordinary in them. Mr. Guzman said he estimates you are reading at a college level. That's essentially the report I got from each of your instructors, with the exception of our physical education instructor, Mr. Lawson, who said he had a long road ahead with you."

He closed the file. Leaned forward slightly. "So what's different?"

Maybe I didn't think far enough ahead on this. I thought maybe they'd just give me some more interesting work. Time to think up a lie, and think it up quick. It's always easier to convince people of what they want to believe. He wants to believe he's running a school that's superior to a public school.

"There was no reason to try at my old school. If I ripped through *Fun With Dick and Jane,* so what? They didn't have any idea what to do with me. I thought you might."

Hartfield's face remained impassive. "We've got a few options." He held up three fingers and began ticking them off. "One, we can leave you alone and let you be just as bored as you must have been in your last school. Two, we can use you to tutor the other students, at least in every class other than PE. Three, we can design a special course of study just for you. You don't need an elementary or junior high education. Hell, I'm not sure you need a high school education. I promise you this. You may be smart, but I've got instructors who are smart, too, and they've been around a lot longer than you. So, what do you think?"

"I know it's not up to me, but I'd rather have the special course of studies. Keeping me going on the same material is a complete waste of time. Having me tutor the other Turtles is fine, but it's not natural. Eventually, someone will resent me being put in a position over them. As you mentioned, I'm nothing special physically, so if someone wanted to bully me, they could, pretty easily. If I had my own course of studies, could I stay in with my class? Be with them, but just do different work?"

"In most cases, yes. We might want to take you out in a few cases for lectures or explanations, but most of the time, I think we can leave you in your classroom. Why?"

"Because I think I probably can help some of the other Turtles, if it's not rubbed in their face. Maybe the best thing to do would have me skip PE each day? I could meet with whoever you wanted then."

The ghost of a smile crossed Hartfield's lips. "Don't try to fool an old fool, cadet. I think that PE class is the one you need the most. In fact, since it's your last class of the day, I'll ask Mr. Lawson if he'd mind staying after class for half an hour or so to give you some extra work."

Michael grimaced.

"You don't play an instrument, do you? We can always use another clarinetist or tuba player for the Hartfield Marching Band."

No thanks, I was perfectly capable of being ostracized without picking up a tuba.

"No, sir. No musical talent in my family."

"Fine, fine. We'll make everything else work. For today, just continue on with your regular studies. We'll have your new program in place soon enough. Dismissed."

Chapter Thirty

One week into the new school year, the first Turtle wet his bed. His name was Will Summers, and he didn't broadcast it. He did everything to he could to cover it up. Pusser had a sharp nose, though, and soon found the soiled sheets underneath the perfectly made blanket.

He pointed to the yellow stain and shouted, "Whose bunk is this?" even though he already knew. The boys standing around Will took an imperceptible step back. Pusser homed in on him. "Is this your bed, cadet?"

A small, miserable nod.

"Bed wetter, eh? Well, we have a solution to that here at Hartfield Academy." In one smooth motion, he pulled the blanket and sheet off. He crumpled the messy sheet into a ball, then said, "Come here, cadet."

Will hesitated, took one step, then hesitated again.

"*Now,* cadet."

When Will was close enough, Pusser threw the balled-up sheet at him, catching him in the face. "You will carry this sheet with you, wherever you go today. I will come looking for you, and if you are not carrying it, then you will carry it with you for a week. Understood?"

Will's eyes brimmed with tears, but he looked down, hoping no one would notice.

Dominick pushed forward from the back of the barrack. "Lieutenant Pusser, sir, is that really necessary? No one would do this," he pointed to the sheet in Will's hands, "on purpose, and humiliating him doesn't do any good."

Dominick braced for an explosion. He was the strongest and fastest Turtle, but standing a few feet away from Pusser, the differences were obvious. He was a child. Pusser was a boy in maturity, but a boy in a man's body.

Pusser didn't explode, though. Instead, he smiled broadly, which showed an extra tooth that had grown in over his right canine. He strolled up to Dominick, stood six inches away from him and spoke down into the top of his head. "Davidner, right?"

Dominick nodded into Pusser's breastbone.

Pusser laid a hand casually on Dominick's shoulder. "Where's your bunk, Davidner?"

Staring straightforward, Dominick pointed toward the back of the barrack.

"Top or bottom?"

"Top."

"Excellent." Pusser snap-turned and strode to the back of the barrack, where he removed Dominick's sheet and blanket, again in one smooth pull. He dropped them on the concrete floor, unzipped his uniform pants, and urinated a steady stream on them. He sighed, a small "Ahh," of pleasure, then replaced the soggy blanket on the top bunk, wadded the sheet up and walked back until he was standing directly in front of Dominick again. He pushed the sheet against Dominick's chest hard enough to make him take a step and a half back.

"Same rule for you. If I catch you without your sheet, you'll carry it for a week. I know, I know, you all think I'm an asshole because I make you do this, but this is the way it's been at Hartfield since the beginning. Hartfield turns boys into men, and men do not piss in their beds. Now. Anybody else got an opinion about this?"

Goddamn, I hate bullies.

Feeling like he was in a fever dream, but powerless to stop himself, Michael pulled his sheet off his own bunk. *What the hell am I doing?* He unzipped his own pants, peed on the sheet, then made his way to stand beside Dominick and Will. Will looked grateful. Dominick whispered, "I knew you had it in you."

Pusser towered over Michael and shook his head. "They told me you was some kind of genius, but I've never seen a genius piss on his own sheets before. Any other idiots want to join the moron parade?"

It wasn't like the scene in *Spartacus* where everyone leapt forward at once, but eventually, Jimmy Markson and Pete Wemmer took their sheets off, urinated on them, and got in line. When they lined up for breakfast, five Turtles carried their sheets with them.

On the way to the cafeteria, Pusser heard it from the older cadets.

"You must be the world's worst babysitter, Pusser!" and, "Where's your sheet, Pusser?" and, "Toilets broken in your barrack, Pusser?"

TYPICALLY, 6 P.M. TO 9 p.m. was study time. When the Turtles filed in after dinner, five of them still carrying their sheets, Pusser was waiting for them.

"I don't know what you little idiots thought you were up to today, but it stops here, got it? Any more of this 'all for one and one for all' shit, and I will make your lives hell. All of you head to the laundry room. You can sit in there and study until your sheets don't stink any more. Then, hightail it back here. Understood?"

All five nodded, snapped off a salute, and marched to the laundry room. Once there, they piled all the sheets into a single industrial washing machine, poured the soap in and started it.

Will Summer looked at the other boys. "Sorry guys. This is my fault."

Dominick laid an arm across his shoulders. "It's no big deal. If we weren't doing this, what would we be doing? Homework? I'd rather be hanging out with you guys than doing that."

"I still feel bad ..."

"It's no big deal," Dominick said. "Could have happened to any of us. If it wasn't you, it would have been somebody else. I just don't like bullies."

"And that's exactly what Pusser is—a bully," Michael said.

"Yeah, but he's *our* bully, right?" Jimmy Markson asked, with a laugh.

"I guess so," Dominick said. "We're stuck with him, right?"

"Probably," Michael said. "Even if we got rid of him somehow, whoever we get next might be even worse. Pusser's a bully, but he's stupid, so we should be able to manipulate him. Someone else might be smarter."

"The genius speaks," Dominick said. Michael flushed, but Dominick continued, "He's right. If we can just get Pusser to be more of a human being, that's probably better than killing him." He looked around at the other boys with a wink. "Just kidding. He hasn't done anything bad enough for me to kill him. Yet."

The washing machine tumbled and rinsed noisily.

After a minute's silence, Will finally said, "Anyway, I appreciate you guys standing up with me. You didn't have to do it." He changed the subject. "So, how'd you guys all end up here?"

Pete Wemmer, who rarely spoke, said, "I had no chance of going anywhere else. Third-generation Hartfield. My dad's been talking about me coming here since I was born."

"Me, too," Jimmy Markson said.

"Not me," Dominick said. "I pissed my old man off so bad that he's making me come here."

"What'd you do?" Will asked.

Dominick leaned in toward the rest of the boys, lowering his voice. "He's got this old Dodge that he's been working on fixing up. It's been up on blocks in his shop for years. Finally, this summer, he got it running. One day when he was at work and Mom was at the store, I took it for a spin."

"Whoa," Jimmy said.

"Yeah, whoa. It was pretty cool, but I had a hard time reaching the pedals and seeing out the windshield at the same time. I ended up running it through our neighbor's yard and into their shed."

The other boys winced. Dominick shrugged. "Totally worth it." He looked at Michael. "What about you, genius. How'd you end up here?"

It was Michael's turn to shrug. *My father's a pervert, so I killed him until I got tired of killing him, then hurt him the worst way I knew how, and now I'm here.*

"My parents thought I wasn't living up to my potential, and that I needed a little more discipline, or whatever, so here I am. This place isn't the greatest, but most of the time it's better than home."

"If this place is better, then home must really suck," Will said. "I just liked to skip school and hang out with my friends a lot. They told me if I skipped one more time, they were gonna send me away to military school. I didn't believe 'em. Guess I do now."

Will looked so downcast at this conclusion, it made the other boys laugh.

Dominick biffed him in the shoulder. "Cheer up." He looked around at the four other boys. "We are the Turtles, the mighty, mighty Turtles, right?

Chapter Thirty-One

Things got tougher for the Turtles, especially the five boys who had challenged Pusser's authority.

Every day, Pusser found some reason to punish one or more of them. The punishments started small—cleaning the latrine—and escalated to physical tests of pain and endurance.

Pusser added new barrack rules weekly. Boots must be laced in a specific manner and put toe-first under the bottom bunk prior to lights-out. Beds must be made in the morning so tightly that a quarter will bounce off the top. All clothes must be folded and stored in the proper order in the footlocker.

Lieutenant Pusser prowled the barracks each morning, an eagle-eyed predator on the hunt. "Cadet Wemmer! Why is there a sleeve protruding from your footlocker? Five minutes in deep knee-bend, arms out." Or, "Cadet Davidner, why is your uniform not properly tucked in the back? It's not like I asked you to eat an apple and shit a fruit salad. Just tuck your tails in. Fifty proper push-ups."

The human mind has a nearly infinite ability to adapt to new circumstances, and so it was for the Turtles. They learned each new rule and followed it, only to receive a new rule the next day.

The small group of Michael, Dominick, Will, Jimmy, and Pete didn't take the punishments without giving something back, though. Several of the boys had special talents they put to good use.

Pete Wemmer had an uncle who was a ventriloquist, and he had taught him how to throw his voice without moving his lips. When the Turtles were lined up to head for breakfast, he would say, "Hey, who farted?" loudly, but inconspicuously. While Pusser was striding up and down the line, looking for the troublemaker, he would say, "I think it's Pusser" just as Pusser was walking by him. The toughest challenge for the rest of the group was to avoid smiling and giving themselves away.

Will Summers was a veteran of sleepaway camps and so came armed with helpful information like how to short-sheet a bed, or even better, how to trap a toilet.

Lieutenant Pusser was a creature of absolute habit, the result of eight years of schooling at Hartfield Academy. One cold October night, twenty minutes before lights-out, Will slipped out of his bunk and entered the second stall from the left. Fifteen minutes before lights-out, Pusser grabbed his copy of *Hot Rod* magazine, headed to the second stall from the left, and closed the door, just as he did every night.

A minute later, his cry of, "Holy shit! What the hell?" echoed through the barrack.

Will had stolen enough clear plastic wrap from the kitchen to wrap the entire bowl.

Pusser came barreling out of the latrine, his underwear splattered with urine.

Pete threw his voice to say, "Looks like Pusser will be carrying his own sheet tomorrow," as loudly as he could. This time, the boys couldn't help it. They not only smiled, they laughed out loud. It didn't matter, though, because the rest of the Turtles had joined in.

They all ended up cleaning the latrine top to bottom and doing an hour of calisthenics in the barrack. They all agreed, in the words of Dominick Davidner, that it was "totally worth it."

THE THIRD WEEK OF OCTOBER meant the Hartfield Game. Some parents and graduates came for the event, but to Michael and the rest of the Turtles, it didn't mean much. Cadets weren't allowed to play in the Hartfield Game, an expansive, all-day version of Capture the Flag, until their fourth year at the Academy, so they were merely hoping for a day off from studying military history, marching drill, and other routines.

It was not to be. At 1100 hours, Pusser gathered them outside and led them in marching in formation around the track.

"You are hopeless. I would be embarrassed to turn you over to another prefect in the condition we're in, so let's march. Then, just for fun, we'll march some more."

Because the Game marked a special occasion, they marched in their dress blues, with a white cap and a decorative sword attached at the belt. As they marched, they chanted.

"Everywhere we go, huh! People wanna know, huh! Who we are, huh? Where we come from, huh? So we tell them! We are the Turtles! The mighty mighty Turtles!"

Michael counted the laps as they marched, four laps to a mile. He had counted twelve trips around and was sure they were wrapping up when a few sets of parents, attracted by their chanting, wandered back toward the track.

Lieutenant Pusser's eyes lit up.

Oh, shit, here we go, then.

They continued to march until every parent had walked away.

Chapter Thirty-Two

"I'd rather punish twenty-four innocent boys than let one guilty boy get away with something," Pusser said. He was standing in front of the barracks, red-faced and sputtering.

Someone had snuck into Pusser's footlocker, stolen all his underwear, dyed it bright red, then replaced it.

He'd had the Turtles standing at full attention for fifteen minutes. "I don't care if a fly takes a two-pound shit on your eyelid, you do not move while you are at attention. We will stay like this until someone confesses."

No one did. Michael knew who had done it, of course. He had been in on the planning and had distracted Iggy in the kitchen while Will had stolen the food dye from the cupboard. He had stood guard at the laundry while Pete had washed, dried, and folded the underwear before sneaking it back into the footlocker during lunch break.

For the first time in two lives, Michael Hollister had friends. He still didn't trust it, and thought it could evaporate at any moment, but being part of a group gave him a feeling of belonging that he'd never known.

"So, here's how it's going to happen. Either the little idiot who ruined my personal belongings will step forward and take their punishment like a man, or every Turtle will be out on that track running laps."

A groan erupted from every corner of the barracks. Outside, the wind was whipping, rain was flying sideways, and temperatures had dropped into the upper thirties. No one wanted to spend a moment outside, let alone run laps in weather like that.

Maybe we should have thought this through a little better. Should have known this would push Pusser too far.

Michael glanced at Dominick beside him. Dominick shrugged his shoulders, twitched his mouth. Pusser saw it out of the corner of his eye and pounced.

"Davidner. Hollister. I should have known. It's always you two little shits, isn't it? I'm gonna stick my feet so far up your asses, I can wear you like slippers."

"Sorry, Lieutenant. It's not Michael, it's just me. I thought red was your favorite color, so I was just trying to help."

Michael opened his mouth to speak, but Dominick caught his eye and warned him off.

"Davidner, you are making me believe in reincarnation, because no one could get this stupid in one lifetime. You expect me to believe you managed this all on your lonesome? Because I'm not sure you're smart enough to wipe your own ass, let alone do something like this."

Dominick quickly looked down.

"Laps, Davidner. Lots and lots of laps. You are ruining my perfect evening by making me go outside in this god-awful storm, so I am going to ruin your night by adding a few more laps. It's colder than a well-digger's butt out there, so I'm going to get bundled up and stay nice and warm. I want you to change into your T-shirt and shorts."

Dominick's head snapped up. "Seriously, Lieutenant?"

"Seriously, cadet. You've got two minutes to get changed while I bundle up. Move."

As soon as Pusser went away, Michael said, "This is too much, man. We've got to tell him you didn't do this by yourself."

"Sure, then there can be five of us freezing our testicles off out there, instead of just me. Forget about it. I'll do it."

Pusser, dressed in his winter coat, gloves, and hat, and Davidner, dressed for a warm summer day in T-shirt and shorts, left the barracks.

Michael looked at Will, Jimmy, and Pete and said, "I can't sit in here while he's out there running for us. I've got to go, too."

In short order, every Turtle had grabbed his coat and headed to the track. As soon as they hit the exterior door, a blast of frigid Northern California November wind hit them in the face.

"Oh, shit," Pete muttered. "He won't really make Dom run in this, will he?"

"He's a pissed-off sadist with power behind him. Of course he will," Michael answered. "Let's go."

When the Turtles arrived at the track, Pusser was stamping his feet, trying to stay warm. Dominick was on the far side of the track, already soaked through, keeping a steady pace.

"Holy shit," Michael said. "He's gonna kill him." He walked to stand beside Pusser. Michael barely came to his shoulder.

I hate being this size. How do I ever get anybody to take me seriously when I'm so small?

"Lieutenant Pusser?"

"What, cadet? Why the hell are you guys out here? You should be in the barrack, studying."

"It wasn't just Dominick, sir. It was me, too."

"I know."

"Sir?"

"It was Dominick, you, Summers, Wemmer, and Markson. It's always you guys. You think I'm stupid, I know. And, maybe next to you I am. Unlike you, I'm not an idiot, though. Every time anything goes wrong, it's you guys."

Just then, Dominick passed in front of where they were standing. He flashed Michael a quick grin, then focused on putting one foot in front of the other.

"You're right. Can we call a truce?"

"A truce? Haven't you studied military history yet? A truce is called when it is beneficial to both parties who are approximately equal in strength. You guys are a bunch of little pissants that need to be taught a lesson. I'm just the guy to do it."

Michael nodded. "Okay."

He stepped away, stripped off his coat, and was immediately soaked by the pounding rain. He shivered, then stepped onto the track.

"Hollister, what are you doing?"

"Running, sir."

By the time he got to the first turn, Dominick had caught up to him.

"Michael, what the hell?" he yelled over the wind.

"Can't stand to see you having all the fun."

What's the worst that could happen? Catch pneumonia and die? Would I just start over again, wake up back at home in bed?

Dominick and Michael completed the first lap together, albeit at a much slower pace than Dominick had run on his own. When they passed the start/finish line, Will, Jimmy, and Pete had all shucked off their coats and were waiting for them, smiling and shivering.

Each lap around became slower, but they kept going, pushing through the wind and the rain. The rest of the Turtles, who sometimes resented the closeness of the five runners, cheered them each time they passed.

Finally, after a full hour had passed, Pusser stood in the middle of the track and held up his hands. "That's it. Head inside. And, if any of you ever touch my stuff again, I will rip off your heads and shit down your neck. Got it?"

The five nodded weary agreement. On the way inside, those who had originally been wearing coats picked them up, now heavy with rain. Back inside the barrack, they headed immediately for the communal showers. The warm water sent tingles of pain at first, but warmed them up quickly.

"We're probably all gonna be deathly sick tomorrow, right?" Jimmy asked.

"Nah," Michael said. "We're tough, right?"

"Tougher now," Pete said.

Michael called a huddle while the water still ran, covering their voices. "I think we've pushed him about as far as we can."

"Right, so what's next? Maybe that'll push him over the edge," Dominick said. He was dead to the world but always ready for another battle.

"No, no more. Somebody's gonna get hurt if we keep it up."

"You mean, just give up?"

"Let's just give it a rest, okay, Dom?"

Dominick shrugged. "I guess, if you say so. You're the genius."

Chapter Thirty-Three

Carrie sat, chin in hand, watching Michael Hollister living his new life. She had learned that by manipulating her pyxis, she could follow him back, even into his previous lives. She took it far enough back to see his abuse in prison, but stopped there.

I guess he was punished pretty badly for what he did to me. She chose not to rewind any further. She did not want to witness herself being murdered.

She soon figured out that the colors at the edge of the picture the pyxis generated related to the amount of emotion Michael was feeling. When she had first seen him, lying in bed, sobbing into his pillow, the outer frame of the picture had been a golden white. While he was being attacked in the prison, or when he was dumping the bucket of water on the boy in the bathroom, it was the same.

It doesn't matter whether the emotion is good, bad, or horrible, it all counts the same. This is a messed-up system.

Ever since Michael's first breakdown, muffling his sobs in his bedroom in Middle Falls, the color around the frame had gone a dark gray, where it stayed most of the time.

Guess he doesn't feel much emotion unless he's killing someone, or doing something else evil.

I think I'll go crazy if I have to sit here, watching him feel happy about hurting other people for the rest of his life.

A new picture dropped down over the top of her view of Michael. It was another young boy. He had dark, curly hair and a smile on his face. He was running around a track. The boy laughed, and the frame around him was bright white.

New blood, I guess. Good. Maybe this boy will be worth watching. Maybe I can actually do something to help him.

Carrie touched the pyxis and an information file dropped down. She read with interest.

Chapter Thirty-Four

The five boys knocked off their pranks and stopped cutting up and disrupting barrack life. Wemmer even quit doing his ventriloquism every morning in lineup.

For a time, it didn't matter. Pusser still found reasons to ride them, punish them. For a few weeks leading up to Christmas break, one of them had latrine duty, dishwashing duty, or laundry duty, every single night. If anything went wrong, Pusser assumed it was them. Eventually, things settled.

The first week of December 1966, everyone's attention turned to finals and the upcoming Christmas break. Most of the Turtles were excited for the holidays. None of them had ever been away from home for more than a few weeks. After three and a half months, hearth and home had taken on the nostalgic glow of a Frank Capra movie.

The boys were all required to send a letter home every week. Michael neatly folded a blank piece of paper each time, put it in an envelope, sealed it, and sent it off. The other boys filled their letters with reports on their schoolwork and activities, and shared what they might like to find under the Christmas tree. GI Joes and their accessories were popular wishes, as were racetracks with electric cars. Dominick asked for a real .22 rifle. The opinion of the other Turtles was that his parents would never be so foolish as to put a gun in his hands, ever.

School let out for two and a half weeks on December 15. As the date approached, Michael asked for an appointment with Commander Hartfield. He was rebuffed. Commander Hartfield didn't see cadets unless he sought them out. Captain Peterson did agree to speak with him, though.

Michael pushed open the door to Hartfield's outer office just after 5:30 p.m. Supper was finished and he had half an hour of free time before he had to be in the barrack to study. His workload had accelerated slowly but surely since that first week of classes. He knew he was doing work the equivalent of a college freshman, which suited him perfectly, since that's what he was, albeit in an eight-year-old body.

The windows behind Peterson's desk were black. Darkness fell early leading up to the winter solstice. As always, Peterson was working—typing industriously. When Michael entered, he held one hand up for a moment, then resumed typing. A minute later, he stopped, rolled the paper out, and added it to a stack on his desk.

He looked at Michael but did not ask him to sit down. "Cadet Hollister. What do you need?"

"Sir, the Christmas break is just a few days away. Is it possible for me to stay here over the break?"

"Impossible, cadet."

"If it's a matter of meals and such, I could easily make do with MREs for a few weeks. It might be good training."

"As I say, it's impossible, cadet. The entire school is shut tight for two and a half weeks. Even Commander Hartfield won't be here. The gates will be locked; the lights and heat will be turned off. It's unfit for human habitation during those two weeks. The idea of leaving a first-year cadet here is, as I say, impossible."

Michael stared out the window into the blackness for a long moment, then met Peterson's eyes. "Thank you, Captain. My parents will not be coming to get me. Is it possible for someone to give me a ride to the bus station?"

"I'll check the bus schedule and make arrangements for you," Peterson said, making a note in an open notebook. "Dismissed."

Michael saluted, snap-turned and left.

Shit. Two and a half weeks with Father and Mother. They thought this place would be hell, but it's been better than home in every way. Is there any way I could pretend to leave, then sneak back in here?

He turned the idea over in his mind but saw almost immediately that it was useless.

I'll be home for Christmas.

Shit.

Chapter Thirty-Five

The canopy was on the Jeep as Curt and Michael reversed the path of their initial meeting five months earlier, but it was still teeth-chattering cold for the ten-minute drive through the early morning mist. When they arrived at the gas station to meet the bus back to Middle Falls, it was only 6:30 a.m. and the station was still locked up tight.

"Seems like this place is never open, doesn't it?" Curt asked.

Michael didn't answer, but reached into the back for his suitcase, preparing to jump out and wait. Curt put a hand on his shoulder.

"Hang on, what's your hurry? I can sit here with you for a few minutes until your bus gets here."

Michael nodded but still didn't answer.

He had rarely seen Curt since their summer scuffle with George. Curt was in his final year, was head of the student tribunal and prefect of the Ninth Years. It was widely accepted that in another ten or fifteen years, he would return and become commander of Hartfield Academy, like his father, grandfather, and great-grandfather. Michael was a Turtle. There was very little reason their paths would cross at school.

"I get the idea that you're not thrilled with heading home for Christmas."

Michael turned to look at him, and for once, let his eyes remain unguarded. "Peterson talk to you?"

Curt shrugged. "Not exactly. You want to tell me why?"

"No, and it wouldn't matter if I did."

"You don't know that."

I do. I tell you my father has been molesting or trying to molest me over two lifetimes, then what do you do? Nothing, because there's nothing you can do.

"There's nothing you can do. If I could have stayed at the Academy, that would have been great. But I understand why I couldn't, so now I'm going home."

Just then, the bus rolled into the parking lot. Michael jumped out of the Jeep, grabbed his suitcase, and said, "Thanks for the lift, sir."

"Merry Christmas, Michael."

Michael didn't hear. He was halfway to the bus.

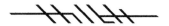

MICHAEL HAD NO IDEA who, if anyone, would be waiting for him when the bus pulled in to Middle Falls.

It's a Thursday, so Father will be at the office. Tess, maybe? Would Mother try to sober herself up enough to drive to the seedy side of town?

The bus trip home was much less eventful than his ride down. No hippies in sight, no sacrilegious songs, no near fist-fight between old lady and said hippy. Michael spent the ride reading *Catch-22*, an unusual book to be stocked in a military academy's library. The librarian, Mr. Snell, had directed him to it. "I think you'll like this one, Cadet Hollister."

Snell was right. He loved it, and his only regret was that he had almost finished it by the time the bus pulled into Middle Falls.

I kind of feel like I'm living a Catch-22 of my own right now. Don't really want to be living this life, but if I choose to not live this life, I get to start over and live more of this life. Lovely.

Michael stepped down off the bus and waited for the driver to unload his suitcase. When he did, he grabbed it, turned around, and almost walked right past his mother.

"Michael!" she said, with a wave.

His eyes widened. Her hair, always perfectly set at the beauty parlor, was more relaxed now, hanging down to her shoulders. The heavy makeup she'd always layered on before leaving the house was absent.

She tried to hug him, but he turned his face away and disengaged as quickly as he could.

"Oh, Michael, it's good to see you. You've grown. And your hair! Your beautiful blond hair is all gone. You do look smashing in your little uniform, though."

That's probably more words than you've spoken to me at one time since I woke up back here.

"Where's the car?"

"Oh. Of course. Right over here."

He waited at the rear for his mother to open the trunk so he could put his suitcase in. A teenage girl walked by, saw Michael in his uniform, smiled and flashed the peace sign at him. "Peace, little soldier man."

Michael ignored her.

On the ride home, his mother chatted more than he could remember her ever doing. She talked about what they were having for dinner—roast beef—what book she was reading—*Diary of a Mad Housewife*—and about the classes she was taking at the local community college.

For most of the trip, Michael stared out the window, ignoring her. Finally he turned and looked at her. *No makeup, no stiff curls hairsprayed into place, no vacant look hidden behind sunglasses. Who are you, and what have you done with Mother?*

She glanced away from the nonexistent Middle Falls traffic and said, "But how about you, Michael? How awful has that school been?"

Have you ever asked me about anything I'm doing before?

"It's fine, Mother. Fine." He turned to look out the window again.

"They send us reports, every month, you know—your teachers? They all say such wonderful things about you. They say you are one of the brightest students they've ever had, and that you work so hard. And that you are even tutoring some of the other boys. I'm so proud of you."

Michael nodded slightly. *You don't get it, Mother. You don't get to ignore me my entire life, then have some sort of attack of conscience and suddenly be my best friend. You can go to hell.*

The car pulled into the long driveway and parked outside the garage. Michael stood silently by the trunk, waiting for his mother to open it. He retrieved his suitcase and headed for the back door. He quickened his step as he approached the door.

Tess. It will be good to see Tess at least.

He opened the back door and burst into the kitchen, a small smile on his face.

A woman was standing in the kitchen. She wore the same gray uniform that Tess always did, but she was her opposite in every other way. Tess was short and round; this woman was tall and angular. Tess was maternal; this woman was distant, if polite. Tess was well into late middle-age. This woman, young.

"You must be Michael. Are you hungry after your trip?"

Margaret hurried in after him. "Oh, I see you met Missy. Missy, this is Michael."

"Pleased to meet you, Michael," she said, then turned her back and went back to work.

"In all that talk in the car, you never thought to tell me that Tess is gone? The one person in this house that cared about me. She's gone, and that's not important enough to mention?"

"Michael! You know that's not right. Your father and I love you very much."

Michael just tilted his head to the side in the universal sign that said, *Oh, really?* He felt tired. Tired all the way through.

"I'll be in my room."

After sleeping in the barracks for so long, his room felt small and suffocating. It was slightly discomfiting to be all alone, with no other breathing, sweating, farting brothers nearby.

He lay down in his bed but couldn't stop his mind from wandering over the months that had passed since he had woken up here in this bed.

So crazy. When I first got here, I didn't know how I would survive the first week. Now, six months have gone by and somehow this all feels normal. Whatever that is.

He looked around the room. Childish things. Pooh. Mickey Mouse. Toys in the toy box.

He closed his eyes. His last thought before sleep was, *I wonder what the other guys are doing?*

Chapter Thirty-Six

Cmdr. Curtis Hartfield sat at his desk, which was almost cleared of paperwork. Captain Peterson and Curt sat facing him. Both had adopted a relaxed attitude. Peterson even leaned back in the chair.

"So, we've got a puzzle on our hands, don't we. He came to you," Hartfield said, nodding to Peterson, "asking if he could stay here, even if it meant being alone and eating MREs. Curtis, were you able to get anything out of him when you took him to the bus?"

Curt shook his head. "No sir. Something's there, I could tell, but he wouldn't talk about it."

Hartfield leaned back in his chair and looked at the ceiling. "I don't like it. I feel responsible for this boy. We've taken him in, he's done everything we've ever asked him to and more, and he seems scared to death to go home." He looked at his watch. "Let's do this. Get Morton to dig into his home life. Take a look at both parents. Dig deep. My gut tells me there's something amiss there."

Peterson made a note on his ever-present clipboard. "Yes sir. I'll do it before I leave."

"Good. Tell him I'd like a full report in the next two weeks. I want to get to the bottom of this."

Chapter Thirty-Seven

The next morning, Michael awoke at 6 a.m. sharp. He no longer needed reveille piped in through the speakers. He got dressed in the unfamiliar civilian clothes, went downstairs, fried two eggs, made toast, poured himself some orange juice, and ate. He had already done his dishes and retreated back to his room before anyone else was awake.

He heard his father go downstairs, get his coffee and leave for the office, but he stayed in his room reading *Midway: The Japanese Story* by Mitsuo Fuchida and Masatake Okumiya. He glanced at the small pile of books on his bedside table and realized he would be done with them well before he returned to the Academy. He would need more to read.

I don't think I could stand to read Mother's trashy books any more.

He went downstairs, slipped his Hartfield Academy coat on and walked to the very back of the yard. He looked at the stump where the tree that had held his tree house once stood. His fingers rubbed the ridges the chainsaw had left behind. The cut was no longer fresh and had begun to gray over.

He tried to summon up some of the anger he had felt that day, but it had dissipated. Destroying the stamp seemed so long ago. Another lifetime, almost. He glanced at Jim Cranfield's porch, hoping to see him there, perhaps performing tai chi, but all was quiet. It was a typical western Oregon December morning—temperatures in the mid-forties, completely overcast, not with rain so much as just moisture hanging in the air, waiting for you to walk into it.

He walked through the gate into the neighboring yard and onto the patio, but saw that the table and chairs had been tucked away somewhere for the winter. Inside, the house was dark.

Shit. How inconvenient that you've got a life, Jim, and are off enjoying it with friends and family.

He returned home and found his mother downstairs in the kitchen—another unusual occurrence. She'd rarely made it downstairs before late morning. Things had been distant between them since his outburst the day before.

"Good morning, Michael."

"Mother," Michael nodded. "Can you take me to the library this morning? I need to get some more books to read."

"When did you become such a bookworm? Six months ago, I couldn't get you to do your ten minutes of reading for school. Now you're devouring books like they are going to disappear."

"No television or anything at the Academy. Gotta do something to pass the time."

"I knew you would be different when you got home, but all these changes ..." She shook a cigarette out of a pack of Kools that sat on the kitchen table and lit it. "Yes, I can take you to the library. Let me get my purse and we'll go now."

As they pulled out of the driveway, Michael said, "Can you just drop me off for a few hours?"

"At the library. You'd like me to leave you at the library for a few hours."

"Yes, please."

"Curiouser and curiouser."

Chapter Thirty-Eight

Michael did his best to avoid his father altogether and was mostly successful. They ate meals together, but there was little conversation around the Hollister dinner table.

Christmas morning was awkward. Michael awoke at six, made his breakfast and retreated to his room. At nine, his mother tapped at his door.

"Michael, honey, come downstairs. We're going to open presents."

Presents. Sorry, Mother, Father. I didn't get you anything. Let's see. What I'd really like is the freedom to never have to come home again. Can you wrap that up and put it under the tree for me?

He followed his mother down to the living room. A Christmas tree stood in the corner, where it could be seen through the tall windows at the front of the house. A rotating light sat on the floor beside it, turning the white flocking red, then blue, then yellow. There was a small pile of presents neatly stacked beneath it.

Margaret picked up a small package and handed it to Clayton, who accepted it wordlessly. She put a present on Michael's lap, then returned for one of her own.

Clayton opened his, which turned out to be a bottle of some European cologne. He set it on the table beside him, took out his pipe and began tamping some tobacco into it.

"Michael, honey, I just wasn't sure what to get you. You seem so grown up now that buying you toys didn't seem right. I thought this might be better."

The package was pretty big, but didn't weigh much.

Michael tore the wrapping away from one end and pulled out an olive drab duffel bag.

"I hope it's all right. I just had no idea."

"Actually, it's perfect. Better than taking a suitcase back to the Academy. Thank you."

Margaret looked relieved and smiled tentatively.

Clayton Hollister finally spoke. "You're not going to need it."

Both Michael and Margaret's heads snapped around.

"What do you mean?" Margaret asked.

"Just that. He won't need ... whatever that is. He's not going back to that place."

To Michael, it felt like the floor was falling away from him. The color drained from his face.

No way. No fucking way you get to do this to me.

"I was a little upset after the incident with the stamp, and I acted hastily. I've changed my mind. Margaret, I want you to get on the phone and do whatever is necessary to get him re-enrolled in school here."

He stood to leave, but Michael jumped up and stood in front of him.

"Come on. Be honest. You sent me there because it was the worst thing you could think of to do to me. You sent me there so you didn't have to see me anymore. Now, you get reports from my teachers that I'm doing well, that I'm fitting in, that I have friends, and so you want to yank me back here. I ... I ..."

"You'll what, Michael? Kill me in my sleep? I had a security door and new locks installed on our bedroom while you're away. It's a shame to have to do something like that, but it's the price of having a mentally ill child."

Clayton smiled.

Michael turned and ran through the kitchen, up the stairs and into his bedroom. Tears of frustration and rage ran down his cheeks.

Now what? Just now *what?*

Chapter Thirty-Nine

Curtis Hartfield III turned the car off Highway 101 and into Hartfield Academy. Max was asleep in the back seat; Curt looked out the window at the trees lining the long driveway.

"It's good to get away, but I'm always glad to get back," he said.

Curt nodded and smiled. "Let's be honest. You're never really happy unless sitting behind your desk, making things run smoothly."

"True enough, I suppose. Ever since your mother died, the Academy and you boys are all I care about. I'm sure the shrinks would tell me that's not healthy. That's why we don't have any shrinks on staff here. Besides which," he waved his hand expansively at the grounds and buildings, "I want to leave this for you, just as my father left it for me, if not maybe a little better."

"Grampa's spinning in his grave, just hearing you say you could do something better."

Hartfield pulled the car around the darkened concourse and parked in front of the Great Hall. "Can you help get Max into bed? I just want to pop into the office and see if there are any messages."

"Sure Dad, 'pop in' and do five or six hours' work." Curt met his father's eyes and said, "It's no big deal. I'll take care of Max. Go to work."

Hartfield smiled an acknowledgement and unlocked the heavy door that led into the hall. A swirl of mail had been pushed through the mail slot. He gathered it up and made his way to the door to the outer office. Inside, he flipped the light switch, blinked, and walked to Peterson's desk. He started to set the pile of mail on his desk but noticed a large white envelope with a label that read "Morton Investigations." He plucked that one out, dropped the rest, and went into his own office.

Out of long habit, he did a quick walk-through of the room, making sure everything was undisturbed. He tossed the envelope on his desk, then sat down and tore off two weeks of the desk calendar's pages, leaving today's date: December 31. A white light on his phone blinked steadily, indicating messages were waiting. He picked up the receiver, heard a stuttering dial tone, then dialed the number to retrieve the messages.

He listened to the first three, taking quick notes on his pad. The fourth played.

"Hello? This is Clayton Hollister. My son, Michael, will not be returning to school after the new year. His mother and I have decided that it is best for him to return to our public school here in Middle Falls. We have paid his tuition for the year in advance. Please have your accounting department send a refund for the unused portion to our address on file."

"What the hell is he up to now? Why wouldn't he want Michael to come back here, when he's doing so well?" he muttered to himself.

His eyes fell on the envelope. He slit one end open with the letter opener shaped like a saber and shook the contents out on his desk. A hand-written letter, plus an official-looking sheaf of papers. The letter was short: "Curtis, this took some digging. Someone didn't want this to be found—Mort."

The documents, stapled together, told a story in themselves. Some pages were stamped "Springfield, Oregon, Sheriff's Department." Others, "Court of Springfield County, Oregon." The pages bore different dates. They began with an interview sheet produced by an under-sheriff who had interrogated a twenty-two-year-old Clayton Hollister regarding the molestation of a six-year-old boy, as reported by the boy's mother, dated August 10, 1951. They ended with a sentencing document, dated November 17, 1951.

The sentencing document mentioned a guilty plea by Clayton Hollister, saving the county the trouble of a trial. The judge ordered Hollister to serve three years' probation, after which the file was to be sealed.

"I'll never know how he manages to ferret this stuff out, but if there's something to be found, he will," Hartfield said, again to himself.

Just then, he heard footsteps. He looked up to see Phillip Peterson opening the door into the outer office.

"Can't stay away either, huh, Phil? You don't report for duty for two days yet."

"There's only so many days I can sit around with my relatives before I go stir-crazy. After a while, filing and going over reports here starts to look better and better."

"Since you're here, can you find Curt? I'm sure he'll be in my quarters, with Max. Let him know we've got to make a trip up to Oregon first thing tomorrow morning."

Chapter Forty

Carrie paused her pyxis. She was starting to get the hang of how to operate it, although she hadn't yet mastered moving time forward and back with it.

Something tickled at the back of Carrie's mind, so she spun her pyxis counterclockwise, showing her events back in Michael's timeline. She paused it when the screen turned the brightest white imaginable—the night that Michael was sobbing into his pillow. She backed it up a little more and watched the whole scene unfold. The boy looked so small and helpless.

Oh. Oh, Michael.

Chapter Forty-One

Michael was in his bedroom, but that was nothing new. He had been in his bedroom constantly since his father had told him he was pulling him from Hartfield Military Academy. He came out for meals and to use the bathroom, but nothing else.

This is such a screwed-up situation. I didn't want to go there in the first place, but when it turned out to be great, he yanks it away from me. And what can I do about it? Nothing. I'm still only nine years old. Can't get a driver's license. Can't earn a living. I'm totally screwed.

Michael had skipped breakfast and it was after two in the afternoon, so he went downstairs to make himself lunch. He was heating a can of chicken noodle soup on the stove and making a sandwich when the doorbell rang.

To hell with that. It's New Year's Day. They can answer the damn door themselves.

His father was in the television room, watching a football game. He yelled, "Margaret, get the door, will you? I'm watching the Rose Bowl!"

Michael heard his mother come downstairs and open the front door. "Yes?" she said. There was a note of surprise in her voice.

"I apologize for dropping in unannounced. Is Mr. Hollister home, and can I speak with him, please?"

"Oh! Oh, certainly. Come in. Please, wait here. I'll get him."

Michael froze. *That's Commander Hartfield's voice. What's he doing here?*

He heard his mother walk into the television room, then muffled whispers. A moment later, the television clicked off.

More footsteps. "Yes? What can I do for you?" he heard Clayton Hollister say.

Michael peeked around the corner of the kitchen and saw his mother and father on one side of the entryway, Curtis and Curt Hartfield on the other. The Hartfields were both wearing their full uniforms. Both of the visitors were taller than Clayton, but the older Hartfield towered over him by at least six inches. Curt glanced around, saw Michael peering around the corner, and gave him a barely discernible nod.

"Mr. Hollister, I am Curtis Hartfield from Hartfield Military Academy. This is my son, Curt. We have some important business to discuss. Mrs. Hollister, would you excuse us?" He looked back to Clayton. "Is there some place we could sit and talk?"

Michael ducked back into the kitchen just as his mother passed by him on her way upstairs. When she saw him, she raised her eyebrows and shrugged. He heard the others go into his father's office and close the door.

Clayton Hollister sat back in the swivel chair behind his desk, the Hartfields in the chairs opposite.

"Now what's this all about, coming to my home like this? I left a message for you at the Academy. Is this really necessary?"

"I think it is, yes," replied the elder Hartfield. "I got your message. I drove five hours up here to give you mine. Michael is going to come back to the Academy with us and resume his schooling."

Clayton Hollister sputtered, turned red in the face, then blurted out, "Like hell he is. Who do you think you are? Michael is my son, and he will do exactly what I tell him to do, do you understand? Now, get out of here, before I have to call the police."

"You're welcome to call the police, Mr. Hollister, but there's something you should see first." Hartfield reached inside his uniform jacket and withdrew a sheaf of folded papers. "You're going to want to look these over."

Hollister snatched the papers out of Hartfield's hand, tossed them down on the desk in front of him, then froze when he saw the county sheriff's stamp in the corner. The blood that had rushed to his cheeks suddenly dissipated, and he turned as gray as the Oregon sky outside.

"What ... what ... how did you ..."

"That doesn't matter, does it? Now, if you want to call the police, I am happy to share these reports with them, and I have a strong hunch Michael would have a story to tell them, too. A story that you very much would like to keep them from hearing. If that's not enough, I've made copies of this report that I am happy to share with the other business leaders here in Middle Falls. I'm not sure what this would do to your business and reputation, but I have to guess it wouldn't be good."

Clayton Hollister rose, leaning forward with his knuckles on the desk, and glared at Curtis Hartfield. Hartfield held his gaze. After a few seconds, Hollister fell back into his chair. He looked beaten for a moment, then gathered himself and said defiantly, "You want him? Fine. Take the little shit. Just don't ever expect to see another dime from me. I don't know what you see in that little freak. He's threatened to kill me, did you know that?"

"I'm sure he has. I don't blame him."

"That's fine," Clayton said. "I don't give a damn. I sent him away because I was washing my hands of him. He's all yours." He stood, threw the doors to his study open, and strode to the back door, slamming it behind him. He stood with his back to the house, furiously tamping tobacco into his pipe and attempting to light it with shaking hands.

Still in the kitchen, Michael stood silently. The soup on the stove, long since forgotten, bubbled over with a hiss. He switched the burner off, then turned to see both Hartfields smiling down at him.

"Go pack your bag, Michael, and don't forget to kiss your mother goodbye. We're taking you with us."

Part Three

Chapter Forty-Two
July 1969

For two and a half years, the world continued to turn.

In 1967, the Summer of Love, Woodstock, free love, Haight-Ashbury and *Sgt. Pepper's Lonely Hearts Club Band* came and went without leaving so much as a mark on Hartfield Military Academy. Parents continued to enroll their sons as cadets, believing it was *just what he needs to be a better man*. Those cadets continued to wear their hair high and tight, pledge their allegiance, and learn what honor and brotherhood was. Curtis Hartfield IV, who graduated at the top of the Hartfield Academy class of 1967, was accepted into West Point and began his four years of study there.

The year 1968 began with the Tet Offensive in Vietnam. Thousands of American soldiers died, including two dozen who had attended Hartfield Academy. The entire school gathered on the front lawn each time the death of a Hartfield alumnus was announced. Max played Taps each time, as he was the most talented bugler Hartfield had. In the spring of that year, hundreds of unarmed men, women, and children were killed in an incident known as the My Lai Massacre. Lt. William Calley Jr. was the only soldier court-marshaled in its wake.

Martin Luther King Jr. and Bobby Kennedy were assassinated. Anti-war demonstrations grew in strength and number across the United States. Riots broke out at the Democratic National Convention in Chicago. George Wallace ran for president on a pro-segregation platform.

For the cadets of Hartfield Academy, though, it might as well still have been Eisenhower sitting in the White House. The sexual revolution and the civil rights movement passed by without ruffling a single hair on their crew-cut heads. The cadets wore their uniforms proudly, obeyed orders, and marched endless miles around the track.

July 1969 marked the fourth summer Michael Hollister spent at Hartfield Academy. Unlike that first summer, when he had spent his days laboring over flower beds, he either assisted

Captain Peterson with filing and organizing student records or worked in the academy's library—*the finest military and strategy library outside of Washington DC,* as Max was fond of pointing out.

On July 20, Commander Hartfield brought all the staff still on site into the officer's mess hall. He had set up a television on a rolling cart, and it was tuned to CBS. Iggy had cooked fried chicken, potato salad, and peach cobbler. The tables were covered in red-and-white checked tablecloths.

That evening, Neil Armstrong made a small hop off the ladder of the Lunar Lander and pronounced, "One small step for man, one giant leap for mankind." The men of the academy applauded.

"One very large step for America," Commander Hartfield said.

MICHAEL STOOD ON THE sidewalk, watching the stream of cars as they arrived that Sunday afternoon of Labor Day weekend. If the arriving student was a First Year, he talked to both the student and the parents, making sure they knew where to go first. If a Turtle appeared, he smiled and hollered the barrack number that would be theirs for the year. Mostly he was waiting to see Dominick, Will, or Pete arrive. The fifth of their group, Jimmy Markson, had been forced to drop out of the Academy after his father's dry-cleaning shop had gone out of business.

Dominick was the first to arrive. As soon as his parents' Chevy stopped rolling, Dominick bolted out the back door and ran straight to Michael. "What's up, genius?"

Michael smiled. "Nothin', hothead. It's been a long, boring summer around here without you to help me get into trouble."

Dominick flexed his fingers away from him, cracking his knuckles. "We'll have to see what we can do about that!"

A small, red-headed boy with watering blue eyes walked by them, holding his mother's hand. He only came up to her elbow.

Dominick looked at Max and shook his head. "No way we were that shrimpy when we got here." He stopped, gave an appraising look up and down at Michael, who was at the beginning of a growth spurt. "Well, maybe you, Hollister."

Michael stood up straighter. "Don't look now, Dom, but I might have you by half an inch or so. Oh, hey, you know what we get to do this year, right?"

Dominick rubbed his chin. "Torture another prefect?"

"Well, yeah, that too. But mostly, we finally get to play in the Game."

"It'll be our first year, though. We're gonna be meat."

Michael shrugged. "Maybe, maybe not. I had a lot of time to think and poke around the Academy this summer. I think I've got a plan."

"And this, ladies and gentlemen, is why I like having a genius for a best friend." Dominick slung his arm around Michael's shoulders and headed toward their new barrack.

When they were away from all the other cadets and parents, Dominick glanced over his shoulder to see if they were out of earshot. He lowered his voice. "There's something I've been wanting to talk to you about all summer."

"Yeah?"

"Yeah. I know this is going to sound weird, but, do you believe in ghosts?"

Believe in them? Hell, I am one.

"I didn't used to, but I guess I do now. That's a weird thing to think about all summer. Did you see a ghost in your house?"

Dominick shook his head. "No, not really. It's just ... I know you're going to think I'm crazy—"

"—I already do—"

Dominick punched him, but not too hard. "—but I kind of feel like I'm a ghost."

Michael stopped dead. Quietly, he said, "What are you talking about?"

Dominick shrugged. "It's hard to explain. It's like I've lived this life before."

"Like reincarnation, or something?"

Dominick started to say something, stopped. Opened his mouth again, then shut it in frustration. "You know what? Never mind. It's too damn weird. So, tell me about how we're going to win the Hartfield Game as first-year players."

Michael looked at him for a long moment, almost reached out to lay a hand on his shoulder, but stopped.

I'm the last person in the world to pry into someone else's business if they don't want to talk about it. But, still. Is Dom going through the same shit I am? I've never thought about the possibility that there might be others, too, but why not? Whatever. If he is, he is. If he wants to talk to me about something, he will.

"Okay. You know how the Game is played, right?"

"Sure. Everyone wears flag belts, like a flag football game. If your flag gets pulled, you're 'dead.' Each team has one flag-bearer. When that person gets the flag pulled out of their backpack, your whole team is out."

"Right. So, there are seven teams. Last team standing wins the Game."

"And no team in its first year playing has ever finished better than fourth place."

"Which is why it will be so cool if we manage to win the whole damn thing, right?"

Dom smiled, all talk of ghosts forgotten. He was always ready to fight a big fight or dream a big dream. "Right!"

Chapter Forty-Three

The Hartfield Games were always held the third weekend in October—late enough in the year for the weather to be cold and blustery, but a bit too early for snow.

Many strategies to win the Game had been employed over the years. For the larger, stronger upper years, it was popular to simply surround their flag-bearer and repel any attack with muscle and malice. The younger years tended to hide in the early stages, as they were neither fast nor strong enough to withstand an onslaught. The upper years knew this, and countered the strategy by declaring alliances until the smaller boys had been hunted down and eliminated. Then, they scattered to their own chosen locations and the Game began in earnest. Because of this, hiding spots were like gold, but everywhere a team could hide had been discovered and knowledge of it passed down over the years.

The Game was overseen by Commander Hartfield and the staff of the Academy. Many years, especially in times of peace, former cadets would return to help officiate. In 1967, many of those former cadets were either fighting in Vietnam, dead, or too old to attend, so the officiating was somewhat more sparse than normal.

On the day of the Game, Michael gathered the eighteen other Turtles around him in the barrack, away from the listening range of Doug Brant, their prefect for their fourth year. Lieutenant Brant was perfectly fine as prefect, but all their prefects had been a bit boring after the endless entertainment Lieutenant Pusser had provided their first year. They trusted Brant within reason, but knew that when the Game started, he would be participating on the side of the heavily favored seniors.

Michael had been unanimously voted Turtle Captain for the Game the month before and had been perfecting his strategy since then. The Hartfield Game revolved around strategy, and although it could be adjusted on the fly, each team captain wrote out a strategic battle plan in advance and turned it in to Captain Peterson for his approval.

"Okay, Will," Michael said. "You're the flag-bearer for the Turtles. I have faith in your ability to do the right thing in a tough spot. Dom, you're second in command. If I get taken out, it's all on you. Now, let's get changed into your Game uniform."

Thirty minutes later, Commander Hartfield was standing on the front lawn, a steady wind riffling his steel-gray crew cut. The sky behind him was dark and threatening. The assembled staff stood beside him, wearing crimson armbands to identify them as Game officials. In front of him, broken up into their seven groups, were the fourth-year through tenth-year cadets. The first- through third-year classes stood off to the side. The younger classes playing the Game had a single advantage: numerical strength. The senior class consisted of just thirteen cadets, while the Turtles had nineteen. Michael planned to push this advantage to its utmost.

"Cadets," Hartfield began. "Welcome to another Hartfield Game. My grandfather created the Game in 1919 as a celebration of the first Great War coming to an end. We have held this event every year since, in times of peace and prosperity, and in times of war and want. That means this is the fiftieth running of our game—a momentous occasion."

He turned away from the wind for a moment and coughed.

"The rules are the same as they have been since my grandfather created the Game five decades ago. You may go anywhere on the Academy grounds, but you may not go into any of the buildings. If an opposing cadet pulls your flag, you are out of the Game and are to report immediately to the library. If your flag-bearer loses the unit flag, your team is out of the Game, and all team members will report to the library. The last team that holds on to their unit's flag wins the Game."

He paused, making eye contact with as many of the cadets as he could.

"Over the years, there have been suggestions that there should be a rotating prize granted to the victors. A trophy, or some other symbol of victory." He shook his head vehemently. "Nonsense. We fight for one thing today, just as we will if we are called to the field of battle: honor. Good luck, cadets. You have ten minutes to get to your starting positions. When you hear the bell ring, the fiftieth annual Hartfield Game has begun."

The groups moved away from each other, each according to their individual strategy. The tenth-year cadets marched in formation to the middle of the front lawn, surrounding Andy Tanner, the fastest runner in the Academy, serving as their flag-bearer, and Bob Morgan, the team captain. They snapped to attention. It was a show of strength and a bold statement: *We aren't hiding. Come at us if you dare.*

Michael glanced over his shoulder at the older boys, calculating their initial moves.

They're all using the same strategies they always have. Playing it safe. Good.

The Turtles took off at a steady jog, winding their way through the campus toward the cliff overlooking the ocean. Over the years, many first-time teams had tried to hide out on the trails that ran just below the cliffs, hoping to last as long as possible. The strategy never worked. Teams always dispatched a single fast runner to peer along the edge of the cliff and report back if there were teams huddled there.

Just before they reached the cliff, the Turtles veered off to the left and onto a little-used footpath into the forest. Hiding among the trees was another strategy smaller boys often tried in an attempt to survive, but it was also a loser. If an entire class went missing, the older boys simply called a truce among themselves and hunted the class down until its members were eliminated.

Michael's plan was for the Turtles to hide, but he was gambling he had a spot that wouldn't be found. The footpath intersected a game trail that Michael had discovered long ago—on his first week at the Academy. He had held its location close, never sharing it with anyone except Dominick. They had spent the previous week preparing the spot as much as they could manage without drawing attention to themselves.

When the Turtles came across the sheer rock wall with the ivy hanging down, there was some grumbling.

"We're dead."

"Can you hear anyone coming?"

"Crap, I thought you had a plan, Michael."

Michael smiled, a facial expression that now lived much more naturally on his face than it ever had in his previous life.

Like the Magician in Jim Cranfield's books, Michael swept the curtain of hanging vines carefully aside.

"Whoa," Billy Guenther said, almost in a whisper.

"Yeah, whoa," Dominick repeated. "I told you Michael had a plan."

"Are we just going to hide in there?" Billy asked, a note of apprehension creeping into his voice.

Both Michael and Dominick nodded.

"Are there flashlights in there, at least?"

"No, dummy," Dominick answered. "When they figure out we've disappeared, they're gonna come looking for us in the forest. They'll see a light through the vines."

"So, we're just gonna hide in there all day?"

"That's the plan. Eventually, they'll get tired of looking for us, and whatever alliances they've formed will fall apart. If we get lucky, and they weaken each other enough, we can swoop in and overwhelm whoever's left with sheer numbers."

Billy and several other Turtles looked uncertain.

"It's either that," Michael said, "or we go out and face the Hawks, Eagles, and Badgers head-on."

"Yeah, then we'll finish last, just like every other first-year team," Dominick said. "Is that what you want?"

No answer.

"Come on, then, Turtles." Michael was the first into the cave, followed by Dominick and the rest of the unit. The cave was cramped, dark, dank, and still smelled of long-rotting animal kills.

"So awful! What is that smell?" Terry Jordan asked.

"That's the decaying bodies of the last unit to hide in here. They never made it out alive," Dominick said. "You're next."

"Listen, I know it's not perfect," Michael said. "Dom and I did what we could to get it ready in here. There are buckets that you can sit on if you get tired of standing, but I don't recommend sitting on the floor of the cave. It's pretty gross. And there's a bucket in the corner if you have to relieve yourself. Other than that, stand still, be quiet, and wait."

"How long?"

"At least until dark. By then, they'll be pretty frantic. They'll think we caught a bus into Crescent City or something."

The Turtles pulled their heads and feet into the shell of the cave and waited for predators to pass them by. They sat noiselessly for more than an hour before they heard the first hunters looking for them. That first group passed by at a walking pace, chattering about what they were going to do after the Game was finished.

The hardest part for the Turtles was the cold. They were in, out of the wind, but being so close to the Pacific, the moisture wicked through their coats and settled into their bones. Sitting or standing for hour after hour made them so stiff they felt geriatric. Still, they stayed in the cave and waited.

If they stood at the far eastern edge of the cave, they could see a sliver of light—enough to read a watch by. At 5:15, more than five hours after the Game had started, and as dusk was starting to settle in, a new hunting expedition came looking for them.

It was a group of four older boys, walking slowly, looking under every rock and behind every tree. They had followed the game trail that led right in front of the cave and passed by so close that one of their shoulders brushed against the hanging vines, causing them to swing and sway a bit.

Inside, the Turtles held their breath and gave every effort to blend into the rock itself.

The boys passed on by, two, three, four more steps, but the one who had disturbed the vines stopped and cocked his head before looking back over his shoulder toward the cave opening. He poked one hand at the vines again, then through them, into empty air.

Inside the cave, Michael moved his left shoulder away from the groping hand.

"Hang on a second, guys. I think there's something here."

The other three boys took three steps back and grouped around him, staring at the vines. It was a cloudy late afternoon, and the depth of the forest made seeing difficult in even bright daylight.

The lead boy swept his hand to the left, tearing a handful of hanging vines away and tossing them aside. Inside, nineteen surprised Turtles gaped back at him.

"Holy shit!" the boy cried. "We found 'em."

True enough, but finding them and taking them were two different matters. With a war cry, eighteen of the Turtles—all but Will Summers, their flag-bearer—launched themselves as fast as their stiff legs allowed.

The four boys on the trail were bigger, stronger, and faster, but that didn't matter—they were caught flat-footed. The smaller boys swarmed over them. One of the older boys screamed, "We found 'em!" as loudly as he could, but the four were quickly surrounded by grinning Turtles, holding the other team's captured flags aloft.

"Son of a bitch," the first boy said, hanging his head.

Michael stepped forward. "According to the rules of the Game, you are dead and are not allowed to communicate with your unit." He noticed that one of the older boys held one of the Turtles' own flags in his hand and looked around to see which team member he had lost.

Billy Guenther raised his hand.

"Billy, not that I don't trust the honor of these fine Badgers, but make sure they don't communicate with anyone else on the way to the library. We're going to rebuild the vines as best we can and stay right here until full dark."

Billy nodded, and he and the four much older boys headed toward the library.

Michael waited until they had disappeared down the trail. "Okay, we're not really staying here, but here's what we're gonna do. Freddy, you stay here in the cave, hidden as best you can. We're going to be on the move. If someone is about to capture you here, scream at the top of your lungs how many of them there are. Got it?"

Freddy nodded his assent.

The seventeen remaining Turtles walked down the trail as silently as possible. When they were fifty yards away, Michael indicated a spot where the trail was squeezed between two big rocks. "Okay, split up—half behind the rock on the left, half behind the one on the right. I'm going to stay out here on the trail. When we hear Freddy scream the number, if it's less than five, we'll stay here and capture them as they pass. If it's more, split up, run, and we'll meet back at the cave."

Fifteen minutes later, Freddy's scream of "Four!" echoed through the forest before he was silenced.

Michael stood on the trail between the two rocks, waiting for the approaching enemy. It wasn't completely dark yet, but shadows cast long fingers of blackness around him. A moment later, four more Badgers came up the trail at a full run.

Michael shouted, "Oh, crap!" and turned to run away. Just past the rocks he stumbled and fell to the ground.

He crawled away from the older boys, whimpering slightly.

The four boys slowed to a walk as they approached him. "Wait a minute," the leader said, squinting, "is this the little shit that's supposed to be so smart? He don't look like much—"

The sixteen Turtles hiding behind the rocks promptly swarmed the four boys, relieving them of their flags without a single loss.

Michael stood, dusted himself off, and said, "Thanks, boys. See you in the library." He sent another solitary sacrifice back to the cave with the same instructions he had left for Freddy. The Turtles scattered behind the rocks once again, then repeated the process, taking four Eagles down without a loss.

After dispatching them to the library, Michael turned to the Turtles and said, "It's getting dark enough now that we don't need to play this game anymore. Let's find a dark spot in the forest, hunker down, and we'll do some reconnaissance."

Another hundred yards down the foot trail, they found another small game trail that shot off to the left. Michael knew it was there, but still almost missed it in the dark. He turned the unit down the trail until they reached a fallen tree that had lodged against the lower branches of two neighboring trees, holding it just a few feet off the ground.

"This spot was too obvious during the daytime," Michael whispered to the Turtles, "but I think we'll be okay here for a few minutes. Dom, you're our fastest. Make a scouting run, but don't be gone too long. If you're not back in thirty minutes, we'll figure you're dead and make a new plan."

Dominick nodded and slipped away into the night.

The rest of the Turtles found a spot under the fallen tree, wrapped their coats around themselves and huddled together.

I expect we'll have another raiding party or two before Dom gets back, but with any luck they'll miss us. If not, maybe we can swarm them. And, failing that, at least we've made life miserable for everyone else today.

Half an hour later, now in full darkness, Dominick jogged quietly to the fallen tree. His face was split in an ear-to-ear grin.

"Good news?" Michael asked.

Dominick nodded, and held up his hand, trying to catch his breath. "They must have gotten tired of depleting themselves by sending scout teams after us, so they went after each other. There's only two teams left, and two people on each of them."

"Do you know where they are?"

"Well, I know where they *were*. The two Badgers are just hanging around the flagpole. I think they're counting on the fact that Andy can outrun anyone in the school."

"Any chance you could catch him?"

"None at all."

"Who's the other team?"

"The Hawks. They're both hanging out back at the track."

"Good. We'll have to expose Will to attract them, but it's worth the risk."

"Let's go."

Five minutes later, they were back at the edge of the forest.

"Will, here's all you do. Try to creep along the edge of the forest, like you're scared. Maybe limp a little. Hopefully, they'll see you and come after you."

"It's dark," Will said. "I don't think they'll see me."

"If not, we'll figure something else out. But, it'll be a lot easier if they come to us." Michael stopped, held his breath, and said, "Look. They've got flashlights. That's good. If you need to, step a few feet away from the edge of the forest, so they'll see you. Not too far, though. We'll be right behind you."

Will eased out into the grass, already wet with dew. They needn't have worried about him being spotted. Almost immediately, a flashlight beam illuminated Will.

A shout. Then another flashlight beam, and another, and another.

"I thought there were only two Hawks left?" Michael whispered.

"I guess I missed them," Dominick answered.

"Will," Michael hissed. "Run toward us, now!"

He needn't have wasted his breath. Will had turned back toward them and run, but his feet slipped on the slippery grass. He scrambled to his feet and ran some more, the backpack containing the Turtles' flag flopping from side to side, but the four Hawks were closing, flashlight beams wildly crisscrossing as they ran.

Will found the trail and dove for safety. The four Hawks were so close behind, and running so fast, that Michael knew his plan to strip them as they ran by wouldn't work. Without a thought, he threw himself face-first down on the trail behind Will, yelling, "Dom, get 'em!"

The fastest Hawk never saw Michael and stepped in the small of his back before tumbling into the bushes. The second boy tried to slow, but was too close behind. He tripped over Michael as well and sprawled over him. The other two Hawks went ass over teakettle into the pile of writhing, cussing bodies.

The Turtles descended on the pile, pulling shirts, hair, coats, and, eventually, flags. When the arms and legs were all sorted out, the four Hawks, including their flag-bearer, were captured, along with Michael.

"I can't believe you guys brought your flag-bearer on an attack," Michael scoffed.

The tallest of the older boys shrugged. "It's freezing out here. We just wanted to get it over, one way or the other."

"Impatience has been the downfall of many a military commander. Frozen feet have taken down even more."

Dominick recovered the flashlights. "Spoils of war."

He glanced at Michael, who shook his head.

Flashlights don't help you, they help the other team find you.

Dominick got the message and switched them off. Michael and the vanquished Hawks set off for the library.

Inside, the sudden warmth enveloped them. All the other teams were gathered, awaiting the final outcome.

When Michael walked in, Commander Hartfield was waiting. "Congratulations, cadet. No first-year competitor has ever made it this far."

"Thank you, Commander. It's not over yet, but I'm proud of the Turtles."

There were pots of hot coffee, tea, and cider served just outside the library, but Michael ignored that and found the Turtles who had arrived before him.

"Oh, my gosh, Michael, these guys are pissed!" Billy Guenther said. "They can't believe they're being beat out by a bunch of kids." His face was alight.

Michael nodded but couldn't join in the celebration.

Come on, Dominick. You'll figure something out. You've got the numbers, now.

Half an hour more passed and the cadets in the library grew restless.

The Commander glanced at the clock on the wall. "No Game has ever gone this late," he said to Peterson.

Finally, the door to the library opened quietly and the two remaining Hawks walked in, grim-faced. Behind them, Dominick and the rest of the Turtles raised their hands in victory.

A buzz ran through the room as more than a hundred cadets all started talking at once.

Michael and the small group of captured Turtles ran to embrace the rest of the team, jumping up and down and pounding each other on the back.

Commander Hartfield strode to a lectern that had been set up at the front of the room, flanked by the American flag on one side and the Hartfield flag on the other.

"Settle down now, cadets, settle down." Hartfield's voice, trained by long years of command, carried across the library. The Turtles quieted but slung their arms around each other and looked at him.

"Come in, Turtles, come in. Have a seat here at the front table. It is reserved for victors."

The few older boys who had been sitting there moved quietly away and the Turtles took seats there, with Michael in the middle and Dominick and Will on either side.

Commander Hartfield cleared his throat, then smiled down at the Turtles. "It's been a momentous day, hasn't it? Congratulations to all the cadets, from the first captured to the final ones standing. You fought with honor, and that is the most important thing of all."

Captain Peterson started a small round of applause that eventually spread through the room.

"And in the end, there were only Turtles standing. In the fifty-year history of the Hartfield Game, no first-year competing team has ever won. Hell, let's be honest: none has ever come close. All rise, please, and salute the victors!"

The rest of the cadets shuffled to their feet, faced the Turtles and snapped off a salute.

"As is our tradition, I've had Lieutenant Ignovich make a feast worthy of the day. Please proceed to the mess hall."

Chapter Forty-Four

The Turtles, exhausted but happy, ambled into their bunks an hour later. The older cadets had been quiet through dinner, but the first-, second-, and third-year students had looked at them with a certain awe.

Dominick said, "Okay, Turtles, it's great that we won and all, but you know what? Tomorrow is still Monday, and that means classes—and lights-out."

Five minutes later, all the Turtles were stripped down and three of them were already lying across their beds, sound asleep. Michael was just climbing into his own bed when he heard Billy Guenther say, "Officer present!" loudly as Captain Peterson entered the room.

The cadets who were not asleep scrambled to their feet, stood at attention and saluted. Peterson returned the salute, said, "At ease," and walked straight to the back of the barracks, where, by tradition, Michael and Dominick bunked. "Cadets Hollister and Davidner. Get dressed immediately."

Dominick and Michael scrambled for their clothes and threw them on. As soon as they slipped their boots on, Peterson said, "Follow me."

He led them out of the barracks, across the quad and into Commander Hartfield's office. Hartfield sat behind his desk, still in the dress uniform he always wore on Game day. Standing to the side were three Hawks—Brant, Tanner, and Morgan.

"Sit down, cadets."

Dominick and Michael sat.

"I have a few questions I'm going to ask you, but before I do, there are a few things we need to talk about. What you boys accomplished today was remarkable—something to be proud of. However, if you look at our flag," he nodded his head toward the Hartfield flag in the corner, "you'll see there are three words on it: Honor. Brotherhood. Duty. 'Honor' is the first word on the flag, because without our honor, there can be no true victory. If we lose our honor, we lose ourselves. Understood?"

What the hell is this all about? Michael risked looking away from Hartfield and let his eye slide toward the three Hawks at the side of the room. They all stared straight ahead, expressionless.

Michael and Dominick nodded.

"Good. Now. These three officers of the Hawks have come forth with a serious accusation, and it is important that you tell me the truth. If you do, there will be repercussions, but the situation will be salvageable." Hartfield cleared his throat. "The Hawks are maintaining that the Turtles won by cheating today."

"Bullshit!" Michael burst out, coming out of his chair.

"This will be your only warning, cadet. You will sit and listen, and you will not speak unless I ask you a question."

Michael sat back down, put his eyes on the flag and was silent, but his cheeks were splotched with red.

To the side, Morgan smirked.

"Now, the Hawks are claiming that the Turtles stole their strategic planning guide and used it to win the war. What do you say to that, Cadet Hollister?"

I say they can't beat us by being bigger, faster, and stronger, so they're pulling this bullshit. Typical. Where the hell is their honor?

"Sir, we did not cheat in any way. We never saw their guide." Michael glanced at the Hawks. "Think about it, sir. Their strategy was to put the fastest cadet in the school in the middle of the biggest cadets in the Game and then stand by the flagpole. I didn't need to steal anything to unwind that particular mystery."

Morgan flushed.

"True enough. However, if you had taken their guide prior to the Game today, you wouldn't have known just how ham-handed and strategically inept their plan would be." He looked at Dominick. "What do you have to say, Cadet Davidner?"

"We didn't cheat, sir. We didn't need to. Michael had been planning this for years. We didn't rely on being bigger or faster, we just relied on being smarter than them, which we were."

Hartfield turned to the Hawks at the side of the room. "What proof do you bring? I'm not going to convict these cadets of cheating on your word alone."

Morgan coughed slightly, then said, "Lieutenant. Brant, the Turtles' prefect, brought it to my attention, sir."

Hartfield raised his eyebrows. "Cadet?"

Brant shuffled his feet, glanced at Michael and Dominick, then said, "Yes, sir. After lights-out last night, I was doing my final check, and when I passed Cadet Davidner's bunk, I noticed a piece of paper sticking out from under his mattress. Initially, I was concerned it might be some type of contraband, so I looked closer and saw that it was just a few sheets of paper. Technically, I knew the cadets should not stash anything under their mattress, but it was a minor point, so I let it go."

"And ..." Hartfield said.

"And, that was it. Until tonight. After the Game was over, I was first back into the barrack. Something about what I had seen the night before stuck in my head. I went to Cadet Davidner's bunk, lifted it up, and found this, sir." Brant reached in his back pocket and pulled a sheaf of folded pages. He took two steps and handed them to Hartfield.

The Commander took the pages, unfolded and laid them on the desk. He looked at Michael and Dominick. "This is, indeed, the strategic plan for the Hawks, such as they are. Cadet Davidner, what do you have to say?"

Confusion was etched across Dominick's face. "Sir? I don't know, sir. I have never seen that before in my life. If it was under my mattress, I have no idea how it got there."

"Cadet Hollister?"

"Sir, I have never seen that, either. I think it's a setup, sir. I think they didn't like being beaten by a first-year team, and this is their way of getting back at us."

"Those are serious accusations, cadet, as is the one facing you. Captain Peterson, do you have the records of Brant, Tanner, and Morgan?"

"Of course, sir." Peterson disappeared into the outer office and reappeared moments later, carrying three file folders. He handed them to Hartfield.

With all eyes in the room on him, Hartfield opened all three folders and took his time examining each one. The second hand on the clock behind him swept five cycles before he looked up again. "All three of these cadets have been here since first year. None of them have any black marks or honor issues." He sighed, closed the last file. "I don't like to delay decisions like this, but I need to contemplate what is right. Cadets Hollister and Davidner, I will see you back here at oh-eight-hundred."

Michael and Dominick dawdled a bit after they left Hartfield's office, wanting to let Brant get well ahead of them. When they felt they were alone, Michael looked meaningfully at Dominick, raising his eyebrows.

"Nope. It's a setup."

"Right. I don't get it. The Academy preaches honor, honor, honor. So, why risk so much for so little gain?"

"No answer."

They walked back into the barracks and found that Brant had made himself scarce back in the showers. The Turtles smiled and laughed, waiting to see what the good news was.

Michael held a hand up. "It's not good, guys. The Hawks are accusing us of cheating. They say we stole their strategy essay."

The barrack exploded in indignant questions and cries of "Come on!" and "No way!."

"There's nothing we can do about it now. We told them the truth. We didn't cheat. It's up to Hartfield now. He'll either believe us or he won't. Either way, we know we didn't do anything wrong. We know we won fair and square. That might have to be enough."

The electricity in the air was gone. All the life was sucked out of the room. Quietly, the Turtles prepared again for lights-out.

Michael lay in his bunk and turned the events of the day over in his mind.

Will it always be this way? Work hard, play by the rules, then run into someone who lies and cheats to get ahead? Maybe it was easier when I didn't care about anyone or anything.

Chapter Forty-Five

Michael didn't sleep at all that night, but Dominick had no such problem. Michael could hear him breathing deep and rhythmically, just as he did every night.

If he's got a guilty conscience, he's doing a hell of a job of covering it up.

Both boys decided to skip breakfast and were waiting in the hallway outside the offices when Peterson walked in at 7:45. "Morning, boys," Peterson said.

"Morning, sir," they replied. Michael looked at him carefully. If he knew what the Commander's decision was, he had an excellent poker face.

The boys sat in Peterson's outer office while he unlocked cabinets and drawers and began organizing his day. At exactly 8 a.m., he stood and opened the door to Hartfield's office, motioning the boys to go in.

Inside, Hartfield sat at his desk, folders spread open before him. The boys took their seats across from him without saying a word.

At least I'm tall enough to sit in the chair without having to crawl up into it. Gives me some small amount of dignity, anyway.

Hartfield looked up at them, and Michael's stomach sank.

Shit. He's gonna take it away from us.

"Cadet Davidner. Refresh my memory. How was it that you came to be with us here at the Academy?"

Dominick sighed. "I stole my dad's car, took it for a drive and crashed it into our neighbor's shed."

Hartfield nodded. Like any good interrogator, he didn't ask questions unless he was already certain of the answer. "This car of your father's—did you have his keys?"

Dominick looked out the window, flushed. "No sir."

"How did you manage to start the car, then?"

"I hotwired it."

"Hotwired it." Hartfield's mouth twitched. "Eight years old, unable to see over the steering wheel and reach the gas pedal at the same time, but you knew how to hotwire a car. Is that correct?"

Dominick shuffled his butt around in the seat. "Yes, sir."

"How did you gain this unusual skill so early in life?"

Dominick shrugged. "I guess it's just part of what we learned in the neighborhood."

"I see. Does this neighborhood education extend to an ability to pick locks at a young age, as well?"

Dominick held Hartfield's eyes for a long moment, then broke off and looked back out the window.

"Yes, sir, but—"

"Peterson," Hartfield called, interrupting Dominick in mid-sentence.

"Yes, sir?"

"Where do you keep the strategy reports that the boys turn in ahead of the Game?"

"Locked up in my desk drawer, sir."

"And the outer office door is always locked when you're not here, is that correct?"

"Of course, sir."

"Thank you, Peterson."

"If I asked you to, could you pick the lock and gain entry to Peterson's office?"

"Yes, sir, but I wouldn't."

Hartfield took a deep breath, held it for a long moment, then released it.

"All things considered, including the testimony of three senior boys, the strategy guide being found in your barrack, and given your preternatural abilities in the arcane world of picking locks, I have no choice but to rule in the Hawks' favor and declare them the winner of yesterday's Hartfield Game."

Nothing to be said, then, is there?

"Michael, you can head off to class. Dominick, I need you to stay here."

Michael snapped off a salute to Hartfield, laid a hand on Dominick's shoulder and quietly said, "See you in class, Dom."

Michael Hollister never saw Dominick Davidner again.

Chapter Forty-Six

Carrie sat at her desk, chin resting in her palm. If she'd had gum to snap, she would have been the picture of a bored office worker. In front of her was an image of an older Michael on his bunk. The indicator glowed white, showing he was feeling something, but Carrie couldn't tell why he was feeling so emotional.

Bertellia appeared beside her, consulting a mini version of a pyxis.

"Your early reports are in. You're doing okay, but nothing exemplary. Your scores aren't going to get you universal recognition."

"Is that important?"

"In other words, 'What's in it for me,' right?"

Okay, I'm being petulant.

"It's just that this ..." —Carrie gestured at her pyxis—"is so boring. So repetitive."

Bertellia reached out one manicured hand, hovering over her device. "I could always shake things up for you. Or, you could, if you're so inclined."

Carrie shrank back. "Thank you, no. Last time I did that, I sent Michael sprawling. I'll just sit here and risk not dying of boredom, since I'm immortal."

"This isn't unusual, you know, this sense of ennui."

"Really?"

"Your skill level has surpassed what your workload is at the moment." She straightened, touched her own device. Immediately two new people appeared before Carrie. "There. That will keep you busy for a bit."

I remember sitting at the kitchen table with Mom, once. I made the mistake of telling her I was bored. By the time I got done with the list of chores she gave me, I forgot what bored was. I guess I can chalk that up as another lesson I haven't learned yet.

Chapter Forty-Seven

Michael didn't blame Commander Hartfield for his decision. He knew, with the evidence at hand, it was the only choice he could make. However, that didn't change the fact that he knew they had been unjustly found guilty and punished accordingly.

The day the Turtles were stripped of their win in the Game, Hartfield sent Dominick home. His parents arrived and picked him up before he had a chance to say goodbye. His bunk and footlocker were empty by the time the rest of the boys returned to the barrack.

After that, Michael kept to himself much more. He had trusted Dominick in ways that had constantly surprised him, but he hadn't yet found anyone else he was willing to completely open up to.

EVER SINCE MICHAEL had become a full-time resident at the academy, he had spent Christmas break at the Hartfield family home on Queen Anne Hill in Seattle. It was a sprawling Cape Cod house that looked out over downtown Seattle and the Space Needle.

In addition to the Commander and Max, Hartfield's mother, Madeline, lived there, along with her former housekeeper, Carol. Mrs. Hartfield was in her mid-eighties, as was Carol. When Carol turned sixty-five, Mrs. Hartfield had insisted that she retire, but had given her a room in the house to live in as long as she wanted, then hired a new housekeeper. Carol agreed and picked up a new hobby—complaining about everything the new housekeeper did.

When the Hartfields and Michael arrived for the Christmas holidays that year, Madeline noticed something amiss with Michael as soon as he walked in.

"Well, now, Sunny Jim, what's got your goat?"

Michael smiled wanly, hugged Madeline as he had been trained to do over previous Christmases, and said, "Nothing, ma'am. Just tired, I think."

"Nonsense. No eleven-year-old boy should be tired and so thin-looking this magical time of year. Curtis!" she said, her voice sharpening. "What have you done to our Michael?"

The massive man suddenly looked like a five-year-old boy, and did everything but kick the carpet at his feet. "Nothing, Mother. Just Academy business."

Madeline's hawk-sharp eyes narrowed. "I see. All right, we'll leave that for now. Come in, take your bags to your rooms, then come back down. We've got refreshments set out in the parlor."

THE DAYS AT THE HARTFIELD home passed quietly. Curtis arrived home from West Point for a quick, one-week visit. He, Michael and Max played many games of checkers and Stratego. Max was the reigning checkers champion, but no one could touch Michael at Stratego. In the evenings, everyone played canasta. Michael had never played the game before his first visit there, but he had picked it up quickly. Max was a slow, deliberate player, always considering every card picked up or played. His favorite strategy was to wait until his hands were stuffed with cards, then lay them all down at once, flinging his discard into the pile with a gleeful, "Canasta!"

Madeline mounted several efforts to find out what was bothering Michael, to no avail. Finally, she cornered her son in the living room. "I've never seen Michael like this. What's happening in school?"

Hartfield drew a deep breath, then explained about the Game and the actions he had taken.

"Are you sure you were right?"

"No," he said, shaking his head. "That's the worst part. I'm not sure I was. I know Michael's doing the best he can to move past it, but it's hurt him. He doesn't trust easily, and he feels that I've let him down."

"And maybe you have."

"Yes. If so, there's nothing I can do now."

Madeline reached out and laid her small hand on his large one. "Things always turn out all right in the end. If it's not all right, it's not the end."

Chapter Forty-Eight

When the car returning Hartfield, Max, and Michael arrived at the Academy on December 31, all was dark. They were the first ones back from the holiday. Michael slipped from the back seat with his bag and said, "Commander, thank you for bringing me with you. I know it's a privilege, and I appreciate it."

"Michael ..." Hartfield said.

"Yes, sir?"

Hartfield seemed to grope for words, but came up short. "Nothing. We're glad to have you with us."

"Goodnight, sir. I'm going to turn in. No need to turn the lights on for me in the barracks. I'm going straight to bed. 'Night, Max."

"Night, Michael!"

Hartfield unlocked the front door to the main building, and he and Max stepped inside. "Max, I'm going to check on a few things in the office. Can you go on ahead of me?"

Max turned and hugged his father. He never did that if other cadets were near, and he called him Commander, just like everyone else, if anyone was within earshot. He smiled up at his father. "Night, Da."

Hartfield turned his key in the lock to the outer door, which made a very satisfying "thunk" as the deadbolt turned. "That would be a hell of a lock for a young boy to pick," he muttered. He went on into his office, sat down at his desk, and retrieved his messages.

When the first one played, his chin dropped to his chest. "I'll be go to hell. Now what do I do?"

Thirty minutes later, he opened the door to the Turtles barrack, deserted except for Michael in the far bunk. Immediately, Michael scrambled to his feet.

"Sir!"

"At ease, cadet. Have a seat on your bunk. I need to talk to you."

"Yes, sir."

"For the moment, let's be informal. No need for 'sir.'"

Michael nodded.

What's all this, then? I've never seen him in one of the barracks. He leaves this area to the prefects and other officers.

"Listen, son. I've got something to talk over with you. It might make you angry with me, but we need to talk it out. You've become important to me, Michael, over these last few years, and I hate to lose whatever faith you have in me."

Whatever it is, just get it over with.

"I just got a phone message from Brant's father. He won't be returning to school after the break." Hartfield sighed. "His father said he acted strange during the holidays, and when he sat him down and made him talk about it ..." He shifted uncomfortably. "He told him he was part of something at school that he was ashamed of. Essentially, that he had gone along with several other students to get a cadet kicked out of school."

"Dominick," Michael said, flatly.

Hartfield nodded. "Yes. He said that Cadet Morgan had approached him because he was the Turtles' prefect and forced him to go along with things."

"No one can really make you do something like that, if you don't want to."

Hartfield was silent for a long moment, reflecting. "I suppose that's true, especially from your perspective."

"So what happens now? Does Dominick get to come back?" As hard as he tried, Michael couldn't keep a note of hope from creeping into his voice.

"No. No, he doesn't." Hartfield's eyes met Michael's.

Michael's shoulder's sagged. "Why?"

"As soon as I hung up with Brant's father, I called Mr. Davidner, even though it was so late. I didn't think it could wait until morning. I explained what happened and apologized. I told him that Dominick's record here at the school would be cleared, of course, and offered him free tuition for the rest of the year."

"But that wasn't enough."

"No. Well, not that it wasn't enough, but their family is moving—to New Mexico. I told him that we had a student who commuted from farther away than that, but—"

"But he still didn't want Dom to come back, did he?"

"No."

"Maybe he just didn't like his son being accused of breaking and entering just because of the kind of neighborhood he came from."

Hartfield winced. "I got the idea that was part of it, yes."

Michael nodded. "That's it, then, isn't it?"

"Michael. I made the wrong decision. It wasn't because I didn't trust you. I make many decisions here at the Academy every day. Some of them are going to be wrong. When I do make a mistake, all I can do is take responsibility, make amends if I can, and move on. Obviously, all three boys have been removed from the school. I'll also make an announcement that it was the Turtles, and not the Hawks, who rightfully won this year's Hartfield Game."

"Yes, sir."

Hartfield cocked his head slightly at Michael's insertion of the word *sir*.

"Son, bad things are going to happen in your life. It's inevitable. If I had made the right decision that night, it's likely that Mr. Davidner would be taking Dominick out of school anyway." He glanced up at the stripped-down bunk above Michael's head. "Dominick's?"

"It was, yes sir."

"I know you've had some awful things happen in your life. I will never make light of that. But, this is important—no matter what terrible thing happens to you, your life will be determined more by how you respond than by what has happened to you."

Michael considered that. *Is that easier to say if the person you're supposed to trust the most hasn't betrayed that trust over and over? Or, is it true of everything, no matter how bad?*

"Thank you for coming to talk to me, Commander." Michael stood to salute, but instead reached out his hand to Hartfield.

Hartfield took his hand, then laid his left hand on his shoulder.

"Good night, Michael."

Chapter Forty-Nine
1971

For twenty-one more months, the earth turned, and life went on, except for those for whom it didn't.

In April 1970, the United States invaded Cambodia, and Apollo 13 shot for the moon, missed, but splashed down safely nonetheless. In May, the Ohio National Guard opened fire on students at Kent State University, killing four and wounding nine. Protests against the war continued in cities large and small, and on college campuses everywhere.

In February 1971, American troops invaded Laos. In April, Charles Manson was sentenced to die for his part in the murder of seven people. In July, Apollo 15 landed on the moon and David Scott and James Irwin became the first to ride a vehicle on a surface other than Earth's.

In September, 213 U.S. soldiers were killed in action in Vietnam. One of them was Army Second Lieutenant Curtis M. Hartfield IV, who bled out waiting for a rescue helicopter. His last thoughts were of his father, and Max.

The Vietnam War had come home to Hartfield Academy.

MICHAEL WALKED ALONG the gravel driveway at the front of the Academy, squinting against the September sun. He often walked along this path after lunch. He liked to let his thoughts wander while he looked at the green of the grass, the trees that ringed the front lawn, and the huge American flag against the contrasting sky.

Captain Peterson stood at the smaller flagpole—the one that carried the Hartfield Academy flag. He had his back to Michael, and was slowly lowering the flag. When it reached half-mast, he tied it off and stepped back, looking up at the flag, rustling in the breeze.

Michael had seen the American flag flown at half-mast, but never the Hartfield flag. He walked toward Peterson. "Captain?"

When Peterson turned around, Michael took an involuntary step back. The Captain, the calmest person Michael had ever met, had tears streaming down his face.

"What is it?" Michael asked. "Wait. No. *Who* is it?"

Peterson swallowed, shook his head, then took a deep breath. "Curt."

"Oh. Oh, no." Michael said. His hand had gone to his mouth.

Michael turned and fled, sprinting directly toward the main building. He burst through the door, ran down the hall and pushed his way into Peterson's empty office. Without knocking, he pushed through the Commander's door. Commander Hartfield and Max stood alone in the office. Max had his head buried in Hartfield's chest. Hartfield's face was a knot of pain—acceptance of an outcome he had always known possible, the agony of its arrival. Max looked up when Michael came in and reached his left arm out to him. Michael took a step toward him, not knowing what to say. Max grabbed him and pulled him into the embrace.

Commander Hartfield put his arm around Michael.

No one spoke.

There was nothing to be said.

<hr/>

SEVERAL WEEKS LATER, Curt's remains were delivered to Hartfield Academy in a flag-draped casket, escorted by an honor detail. Commander Hartfield had asked for, and received, a special dispensation from the county health department to bury Curt on the grounds of the Academy.

His grave was dug beside the flagpoles on the front lawn. No heavy equipment was used to dig the grave—there were dozens of volunteers standing by to do the work.

At 2 p.m. on the fourth Sunday in September, Curtis M. Hartfield IV was laid to rest. Madeline Hartfield and Carol had made the trip down and sat in folding chairs alongside the grave. Every cadet wore his dress uniform. His father gave a short eulogy. Commander Hartfield was a man of towering strength and endless vigor, but on this day, he looked only weary and hopeless. His eyes met Madeline's for a long moment, then he stepped to the podium.

"This is my son," Hartfield began, pointing to the flag-draped coffin front of him. "Like me, my father, and grandfathers three generations back, he volunteered to serve his country. In so doing, he knew he was offering to make the ultimate sacrifice. And now, that has come to pass. General McArthur once said, 'The soldier above all others prays for peace, for it is the soldier who must suffer and bear the deepest wounds and scars of war.' I believe that it might be the parents of the soldiers who pray for peace. We should never forget those who also bear the deepest wounds are those left behind to grieve those who are gone."

Commander Hartfield stood back, and Max walked to the grave. Sun glinted off his golden bugle as he played the opening notes to Taps. Every cadet, Hartfield instructor, and member of the honor guard snapped and held a salute. Twenty-four heart-rending notes later, Max let the bugle fall to his side. His face was wet with tears.

The honor guard folded the American flag that had draped the casket and handed it to Commander Hartfield.

Chapter Fifty

Three months later, the school had emptied out for Christmas break and Michael was packing his duffel bag—the same one his mother had given him for Christmas five years earlier. It was scuffed and a bit worn now, as a duffel bag should be.

He was throwing the last of his socks and underwear in when he heard the door to the barracks open.

"Michael? Michael, are you in here?"

Michael stepped away from his bunk and saw his mother. He hadn't seen her in years—since she had come to visit him during his second year at the Academy. She had written him letters occasionally, but he answered only because the Commander ordered him to.

A year earlier, she had written to tell him that she had left his father. That had surprised Michael, because he had been sure she couldn't make it on her own. His memory of her was of a drugged-out woman who rarely left her bedroom. She had surprised him by moving out, finding a small apartment, and enrolling in bookkeeping classes at Middle Falls Community College.

Her hair was a shoulder-length flip. Her skirt was shorter than he had ever seen on her, and she wore cinnamon-colored pantyhose, blue eyeliner, and white lipstick. Michael very nearly didn't recognize her.

"Mother?"

"Oh, Michael, you've grown!" That was true. The last time she had seen him, he had come up only to her shoulder. Now, he was in the middle of his growth spurt and looked her right in the eye.

"Hello, Mother."

"Michael, I know you're planning on going home with Mr. Hartfield, but, well ..." She turned away from Michael and raised her voice. "Jim? Come in, I know Michael will be glad to see you."

A moment later, Jim Cranfield poked his head into the barracks. "So, this is the legendary Hartfield Academy barracks, home of the infamous Michael Hollister?"

If Michael had been surprised to see his mother show up unannounced, he was slack-jawed and flabbergasted to see Jim Cranfield. He looked from him to his mother, then back at him.

Okay. All right. Mother and Mr. Cranfield. I know things have changed in this life, but holy shit.

"I'm terribly sorry to just show up like this, Michael, but I couldn't think of how to tell you in a letter."

"Tell me what?"

"Well, that James and I are getting married." She held out her left hand and waved her fingers, showing off a solitaire diamond ring.

Michael absorbed this.

"Congratulations?"

"Oh, honey, I know this feels sudden to you, because I haven't been able to see you for so long, but it's really not."

"I've been right here, Mother."

Abashed, she took a step back. Her smile faded.

"James and I have been seeing each other for almost a year now, and neither of us is getting any younger."

"A year? Oh, I see. How long ago did you tell me you and Father were separating?" He looked up at the barrack lights as though he was trying to remember. "Wait. Right. A year ago."

Jim Cranfield took a few easy steps toward Michael, his hands in his pockets. "Hey, Michael, why don't you and I take a little walk. Show me the campus, all right?"

Michael hesitated, but nodded. "Be right back, Mother."

Margaret followed them outside the barracks, but veered off toward the front of the Academy, leaving them to walk alone toward the back cliffs.

"Your mother has told me how well you've been doing at school here. When we sat together at the table on my back porch and looked this place up, I couldn't imagine the way things have turned out. That's the difference between real life and the fiction I write. My stories have to make sense."

Michael ignored this. "How did you guys get together? Over the backyard fence?"

Cranfield chuckled. "No, no. I have a confession to make. I wrote a literary fiction book."

"Oh, the horror. Say it isn't so," Michael deadpanned.

"It's to my ever-lasting shame. However, I agreed to give a talk about it at the local library, and there was a very nice turnout. It's an interesting experience, writing books that people aren't ashamed to own up to reading. In any case, your mother was in the audience that day."

"Look, I really don't care, but was all this before or after she left my father?"

"After, but probably not as long after as I would have liked. Here's a life's truth, Michael. We all see our parents as just that: our parents. Not as real, flesh-and-blood people with failings, but our parents. Iconic figures in our lives."

"Oh, I've never had a hard time envisioning my parents as failures. They've given me plenty to work with."

Cranfield's face was calm, but with all trace of his normal joviality gone. "I know that's true, Michael. Your mother has told me. I knew from our conversations that something was wrong in your family life, but ..."

"It's not just my father, you know. She was there every step of the way. She might not have done anything to me directly, but she sure as hell didn't do what any good mother would have done."

Cranfield nodded, looking at the path ahead of them as they walked. "As I was saying, when we are born our parents fill our horizon. As we grow older, that diminishes somewhat, but they always remain large in our lives. Even as old as I am, I still have a difficult time seeing my own mother as anything other than that—Mother. It's very difficult to see her as a real, flesh-and-blood woman."

"So what's your point?"

"Nothing too important, I guess. Just trying to bring a new perspective to you. Shall we head back to meet your mother?" Cranfield waved his hand toward the front of the Academy.

They turned that direction but didn't hurry their pace.

"Forgiveness is a funny thing," Cranfield mused. "So often, we spend time thinking about whether we want to forgive someone or not."

Cranfield stopped and turned to face Michael. "When in fact, the person we really need to forgive is ourselves. Until we do that, whatever else we do is empty. Meaningless."

Michael winced.

Screw you, too. What do you know about it? Why do I need to forgive myself? I was a little boy.

Cranfield raised his hand and gave a half-wave at Margaret, waiting by the car on the front drive. "Ah. Never mind. Don't listen to me—I'm just an old man, given to verbal diarrhea." He gave his best attempt at a hearty smile. "Your mother is going to ask you to come spend Christmas with us. We're driving on down to Monterey for the holidays. She'd like you to come, and so would I."

They walked in silence until they reached her.

"Well?" Margaret looked at Cranfield.

He shrugged. "I'm not sure. I made the best case I could, but I'm a hack writer, not a lawyer. Arguing people from one position to another has never been my strength."

"What do you say, Michael?" Margaret asked. "We'd love to have you come with us. We've got a reservation for two rooms at a lovely little resort that sits up on a hill looking out over the ocean."

Michael looked over his left shoulder, mute testimony to the fact that he lived on a hill looking out over the ocean.

Without rancor, Michael said, "Thank you, Mother, and I know you mean that, but ..." He shook his head slowly. "I'm going to stay here. The Commander's son was killed in action recently, and I want to be there for him and Max, his other son. They need me."

Margaret began to speak, then shut her mouth. A look of pain and loss crossed her face, but she nodded. "This is just where we are, isn't it Michael?"

"I hated you, too, Mother, for a long time." He shook his head. "I don't any more. I know you were suffering, too. I wish you had protected me, but I understand."

"Oh, Michael. I'm sorry. I'm glad you've found Commander Hartfield and his son." She looked him up and down appraisingly. "It's been good for you. You're growing up as a responsible and caring young man."

Is that true? Responsible? Caring? Those are not words anyone has ever attributed to me.

Margaret stepped forward and held him tightly against her for a moment. Michael did not pull away. She held one hand against his chin, and he saw her tears.

I've never seen her cry.

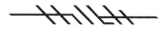

CHRISTMAS IN SEATTLE was a somber affair that year. Madeline and Carol did what they could to keep all their traditions alive, but without Curt there, everything rang hollow.

Even Max, perpetually happy Max, couldn't manage to yell "Canasta!" when he made a huge laydown. They didn't purposefully leave a chair empty at the table for Curt, but it was there.

Chapter Fifty-One
1974

For thirty-six more months, the Earth spun.

In January 1972, a Japanese soldier named Shōichi Yokoi was found living in a cave in Guam, twenty-seven years after the end of World War II. In June, five burglars were arrested in the Democratic National Committee's headquarters in the Watergate Hotel. In November, Richard Nixon won re-election in one of the biggest landslides in American political history.

In January 1973, Nixon announced that the war in Vietnam was over, having achieved "Peace with honor." In May, Skylab—the first U.S. space station—was launched. Meanwhile, televised hearings into the Watergate break-in began.

In February 1974, Patty Hearst was kidnapped by the Symbionese Liberation Army. In April, she was photographed wielding a rifle while robbing the Hibernia Bank in San Francisco. In August, Nixon announced his resignation as president. In September, Cadet Hollister of the Hartfield Military Academy celebrated his sixteenth birthday, making him eligible for a state-issued driver's license in California.

WILL SUMMERS AND THE rest of the Turtles emerged from Lieutenant Iggy's kitchen, holding a single cupcake with a candle burning on it. They sang, "Happy Birthday, dear genius," and presented the pastry to Michael. Dominick Davidner had never returned to Hartfield, but the nickname he had tagged Michael with endured.

Michael waited until the last, off-key note was sung, then blew out the candle, removed it, and stuck the entire cupcake in his mouth—another great Turtle tradition that was met with cheers of approval.

When I first woke up in this life, this is the day I was pointing at. This was the day I could get my own license and make my own way in the world—to escape—if I had to. But, now, I don't have to. He grinned at the Turtles, who were thumping him on the back and laughing at the chocolate frosting smeared across his face. *Now I have the Commander, and Max, and the Turtles. We are not always born into our real families.*

The next day, he made an appointment with Commander Hartfield. Captain Peterson showed him into the office, and he stood straight and tall just inside the office. Hartfield spent another few moments poring over the file on his desk before he looked up.

"Michael," he said, a smile warming his face. "Good to see you. At ease. Sit down, son, sit down."

"Thank you, sir," Michael said, sitting. "I'd like to ask a favor."

"Within reason, if it's mine to offer, it's yours."

"I'd like to borrow one of the academy Jeeps this week. I've been practicing my driving here on Academy grounds, but now I need to take my driving test. One of the Falcons who already has his license said he would drive me into town."

Hartfield leaned back in his chair, steepling his fingers in front of him. "Sixteen already?" He shook his head slowly. "You boys grow too fast. Max, too. He's twenty now."

"Yes, sir."

Although Max was twenty, he would never leave the Academy until his father retired. Now that Curt had been killed, Michael had no idea when that would be, as he had no other heir capable of running the Academy.

"I'm afraid that I'm going to have to deny you the use of the Jeep."

"Yes, sir. Thank you, sir." Michael stood to leave.

"Hold on, cadet, sit down. Don't be in such a hurry. You don't want to take one of our Jeeps to take your test in. They're not exactly built for parallel parking maneuvers. When did you want to take the test?"

"I've got permission from my instructors to be away from campus tomorrow, sir."

"Good. Let's do this. Max and I need to attend to a few things in town, so we'll all head in tomorrow, you can take your test, and if you pass, you can chauffeur us all home."

"Thank you, sir. That's very kind of you."

Hartfield looked at Michael for a long, silent moment, then said, "Dismissed, cadet."

It was an absurdly odd feeling for Michael the next day, as he slipped behind the wheel of Hartfield's Lincoln Continental. He had driven for years, of course, and loved his Karmann Ghia, but that was literally another lifetime ago.

Still, he was able to pass both the written and driving sections of the California Driver's License exam, and after waiting so long, he was once again legal on the road. Another odd thing was, although he hadn't thought about leaving the Academy grounds since he first arrived, now that he had a license tucked in his pocket, a desire to make a trip grew inside him.

Finally, after a month of struggling with himself, he went to Hartfield's office again and asked for permission to take one of the Jeeps on a trip over two days in October. This time, Hartfield granted the request.

On a chilly Tuesday morning, Michael buttoned down the top of the Jeep, topped off the tank at the Academy pump, and set out north on I-5 toward Middle Falls. He kept to the right lane and drove at or just below the speed limit, as though he were in no hurry to actually arrive.

He had thought about, planned, and wondered about making the trip for a month, but now that it was here, he was unsure of how to proceed. He turned off at the first Middle Falls exit and, without a plan, drove to his old neighborhood. Fall was in full swing, and what few leaves still clung to trees were gold, yellow, or brown. Here and there, Halloween decorations dotted the yards.

His old house was the same as ever—white, stately, and unHalloweened. It looked unchanged from the last time he had seen it, almost eight years earlier. He rolled right past it.

No need to deal with you today, Father.

He turned west and drove to Middle Falls High School by memory. Like everything else about Middle Falls, it matched his memory perfectly. He parked directly across the street and stared.

I am a stranger in my own familiar land. Last time around, I would have been in there, getting more and more isolated every day, and becoming more and more pissed off at the world.

A scene ran through his memory. A small church, lit only by a few candles, and a young girl waiting inside. When she heard him open the door, she turned, with a look of anticipation on her face. When she saw it was him, that looked changed to consternation, then fear.

I didn't go there to kill her. I just wanted to scare her. Then, things went black.

Michael blinked away tears. *I'm so sorry, Carrie. You never did anything to me. You were an outcast, just like me, and I killed you.*

The bell rang and a flood of teenagers burst through the double doors at the front of the school.

Would she even be here? Shit, I killed her, but I killed myself, too, and I'm here now.

Michael sat and watched as the flood turned into a stream, then a trickle.

I don't recognize anyone. How can that be?

A small group of four boys pushed out into the autumn afternoon. One of them, an average-looking boy with shaggy hair and a pale complexion, caught Michael's eye.

Tommy Weaver. You little bastard. You put the dog shit in my sandwich. I know you had something to do with my being arrested. Michael's knuckles turned white as he gripped the steering wheel of the Jeep tighter and tighter. The boys walked to the bike rack at the front of the school and two of them unlocked their bikes. They pushed their bikes while the other boys walked alongside. They crossed the street right in front of Michael.

Tommy Weaver glanced inside the Jeep. For the briefest of moments, his eyes met Michael's. There was no hint of recognition, and he and the other boys pushed on past.

Michael watched their retreating backs and waited for his pulse to return to normal. The boys were talking, shoving each other and laughing. Michael turned back toward the school.

I don't even know what I'm doing here. What will I do if I see her?

A tall girl wearing a muted plaid skirt and a baggy green sweater came out of the school. She was alone, holding her books in front of her like a shield, her eyes cast downward. Her long, dishwater-blonde hair was straight and her bangs hung down over her eyes.

Michael's breath caught in his throat, and his hand instinctively reached for the gearshift of the Jeep.

Carrie Copeland walked straight toward him but turned left when she got to the sidewalk. Three boys on bicycles with banana seats and sissy bars approached from the opposite direction. The boys were standing on their pedals, pushing hard. At the last minute, they swerved around Carrie, but the last boy swung his arm out, sending her books flying in one direction and her in the other.

The boy laughed maniacally, shouting, "Hey! Didja see that?" to the other boys ahead of him.

Michael jumped out of the Jeep. Carrie had sat down hard on her backside, but was already scrambling to her knees, picking up books, folders, and papers that were scattered around the sidewalk. Michael ran to her and picked up her algebra and biology books.

He held them out to her. "Here."

"Thanks," she said quietly, not meeting his eyes.

Michael reached out and touched her elbow. "Don't pay attention to them. They're just ... I don't know ... thoughtless, I guess."

Carrie pushed the hair away from her eyes and finally met his look head-on. Michael felt a small frisson—an electric shock of memory, recognition, and nausea, all at once. She pushed partway past Michael once again, but he took half a step to partially block her.

"Carrie ..."

Her eyes narrowed. "How do you know me?" She looked at him more carefully, from his tan Hartfield Academy uniform to his perpetual buzz cut. "I don't know you."

"I know," Michael said, and stepped back. "I just wanted to say that I'm sorry."

"Sorry for what? You didn't run me over."

"I know. I can't explain. I just wanted to tell you how sorry I am."

> For a moment, the veil of non-expression fell away and a flash of good humor crossed her face. "Very well. You're forgiven."

She pushed past and strode quickly away.

Michael stood rooted on the sidewalk.

She forgave me.

Michael hustled back across the street, clambered into the Jeep and turned toward the freeway. He drove a little over the speed limit all the way back to Hartfield Academy.

Chapter Fifty-Two

Carrie tilted her pyxis and moved it slightly counterclockwise. She let the scene play forward, then moved it back, again and again. It showed a tall boy standing on a sidewalk, talking to a girl. Talking to *herself*. But of course, *she* was herself.

It's so unbelievably strange and confusing to watch yourself, to see yourself as others see you. From this perspective, it's easy to see why people felt comfortable bullying me. It was a horrible cycle. Someone made fun of me, I pulled into my shell, which made me an even better target. And the beat went on.

She stopped the rotation and froze the scene. *And Michael. He's tried so hard.*

As she watched, she heard Michael say, "I'm sorry." The color of the surrounding frame was bright white with emotion.

Carrie closed her eyes and did her best to reach out and commune with the young Carrie standing on the sidewalk. They weren't the same person, as each had their own unique spark of the life force inside them. However, they shared a common past, which formed an unbreakable connection.

For a brief moment, she saw two perspectives simultaneously—the view through the pyxis and the view through Earth Carrie's eyes. That dizzying feeling passed, and for a moment, she saw Michael only through Earth Carrie's eyes.

She was able to hold the connection just long enough to take control of the other Carrie's vocal cords and say, "Very well, I forgive you." She saw relief and gratitude flood Michael's face; then she was back at her desk, staring at her pyxis.

She drew a deep, shuddering breath. *I do. I forgive you, Michael.*

Chapter Fifty-Three
1976

A nd the world continued to spin.

In April 1975, the Vietnam War officially ended when Saigon fell and South Vietnam surrendered unconditionally. Paul Allen and Bill Gates founded Microsoft in Albuquerque, New Mexico.

In March 1976, Patty Hearst was found guilty of bank robbery and sentenced to thirty-five years in prison. In May, Cmdr. Curtis M. Hartfield III noticed that he was losing weight.

CURTIS M. HARTFIELD had always been a substantial man. As a young soldier, he had been a muscular tank. As he had grown into late middle age and spent more time behind his desk than in the exercise yard, he had become softer—still, never fat, but solid and imposing.

He was surprised, then, one early May morning, when he felt his pants were loose around his waist. He hadn't stepped on a scale in some time, but when he did, the needle pointed to 215, down more than ten pounds since his last physical.

"Well, I guess my youthful metabolism has kicked in again," he said, squinting down at the scale.

It was not, as it turned out, his youthful metabolism kicking in.

Over the next few weeks, he lost another ten pounds and had to make another hole in his belt so his pants wouldn't slide down.

Finally, sitting at his desk one Tuesday morning, he called, "Captain?"

Peterson appeared in the doorway, clipboard in hand, pen hovering over it, ready to carry out whatever needed to be done.

"Come in, Phillip, sit down." The Commander almost never used Captain Peterson's given name.

Peterson sat on the edge of the chair opposite Hartfield, back straight, still ready to take notes. "Yes, sir?"

"I need you to order me a few new uniforms."

"Yes, sir," Peterson nodded, jotting a note.

"And ... I need them to be a size smaller than what I've been wearing."

Peterson noted that, then looked directly at the Commander.

"New diet, sir?"

"No."

Peterson made another note, which Hartfield questioned with the rise of one eyebrow.

"Just making a note to schedule an appointment with Dr. Crawford."

Hartfield started to object, but closed his mouth and nodded. "Thank you, Captain. That will be all."

IN JUNE, HARTFIELD Military Academy graduated its sixty-sixth class of cadets. They had entered as boys, left as men, and were ready to be soldiers, if they so desired. Will Summer graduated number one in the class.

Michael Hollister had been doing college preparatory work or higher since he first arrived at Hartfield Academy. He had topped out what most of the instructors had been able to teach him by his third year and had begun a career as an adjunct faculty member, tutoring the Turtles and other classes as needed. As such, it was discussed and decided that he would not show in the official class ranking, but would simply graduate "with honors."

Hartfield graduations were held on the front lawn if the weather was willing, and in 1976, it was. The day dawned clear and warm. The stage was set up at the back of the lawn, and the Turtles sat in folding chairs in front of that. Portable bleachers were erected to hold the proud parents, including Margaret and Jim Cranfield, who had married the year before. Clayton Hollister was not in evidence.

Commander Hartfield stepped to the podium, noticeably thinner than he had been even the month before. His baritone voice was still strong. "Good afternoon, cadets, parents and loved ones, and of course," he glanced down at the fifteen senior cadets in front of him, "Turtles." Smiles spread across the front row.

"Welcome to another graduation ceremony at Hartfield Academy. This is always a proud, yet sad moment. Over the last nine years, I've had the privilege of watching these boys grow and mature, to become splendid young men, and wonderful examples of the brotherhood we hope for with each new class. Every class is special, of course, but the Turtles are unique. In the entire history of the Academy, they are the only class to ever win the Hartfield Game the first year they played."

A cheer erupted from the Turtles, along with smiles and pats on the back.

"Enough from me, though. Before we begin handing out diplomas, I'd like to bring up our valedictorian, Will Summer. Will?"

Applause rippled through the crowd as Will, now a tall, strong eighteen-year-old, resplendent in his dress Hartfield Academy uniform, stepped to the podium.

"Thank you, Commander Hartfield, and thank you to the Hartfield Academy instructors and staff who have put up with us all these years. I suppose I should also apologize to Lieutenant Pusser and the string of prefects who followed him for all the terrible things we did to them."

The Turtles cheered again. Staff Sargent Pusser, who had returned to the Academy to see the Turtles graduate, waved in acknowledgement from the podium.

"Seriously, though, every Turtle and every instructor knows that I'm not who should be standing up here, representing our class." He gripped the podium and paused. "Michael Hollister should be."

Michael looked up in surprise, but shook his head vehemently.

"Michael was so far ahead of us, he ended up teaching us almost as much as our instructors did. When we were just scared, homesick First Years, Michael was the calming force that held the Turtles together. The only reason I'm up here instead of Michael is that's the way he wanted it, and that says a lot about him too, doesn't it? Every Turtle could stand up here and tell a story of how Michael helped them out, but we don't have that much time, so here's mine. There used to be a tradition at Hartfield that if you wet your bed, you had to carry your sheets with you all day as public humiliation."

A titter of conversation rippled through the crowd.

"I was the first Turtle to do so, and I was assigned to carry my soaking sheets. First, Dominick Davidner, our brother who is not here, stood up for me; then Michael peed on his own sheets and carried them with him, so I wouldn't be alone. Think about that for a minute. How easy is it to stand by and watch someone else be punished when you are innocent? How difficult is it to put yourself into the line of fire? That's what Michael did for me, and I know he did things just like that for every single Turtle. He did that nine years ago. I'll never forget it."

Will took one step back from the podium and, in a voice that carried to every corner of the Academy, said, "Turtles! Attention!" All the Turtles jumped to attention. They all faced Michael. "Salute."

As one, the Turtles raised their rigid right hands and held the salute for a three-count, until Michael, with tears in his eyes, saluted them back.

Chapter Fifty-Four

The day after graduation, Michael was in Peterson's office, helping him catch up on filing and organizing the applications for the new First Years, when Hartfield said, "Michael, are you out there?" from his own office.

Michael walked to the connecting door, stuck his head in, and said, "Yes, sir. Do you need something?"

"Come in, Michael, sit down. At ease. I just want to talk to you."

Michael sat in the chair he had sat in so often—sometimes when Hartfield was grilling him, like after the incident in town with Curt, or often, these past few years, just to sit and talk.

"So, now that you've graduated, what's next? Do you want to stick around here, or are you off to see what the world has to offer? You've been a tremendous help to us, Michael, and we've never paid you a dime, so if you want to go see what's around the next bend in the road, the school will buy you a car and give you some money to explore. Or, is college next for you? I've been so busy with the Academy, I haven't kept up with that. I am happy to write a letter of recommendation for you."

"Thank you, sir, Captain Peterson already did. I think he may have signed your name on it."

"Ha! That sounds right. I think most people believe his signature is the real one, not mine."

"The truth is, sir, when I first got to the Academy, I was looking forward to the day I would be able to leave, be on my own."

Hartfield nodded. "I understand."

"But now, I see what you do here. You make a difference to so many people, just like you have to me. I wasn't a good person when I arrived—"

"We never saw you that way."

"—and I know I'm still not perfect, but I think I'm a lot further along, now."

"It meant a lot to me that you gave me a chance to find my footing. You, and the Academy, were the first to give me a chance to be a good person. If there's room, I'd like to maybe stay here and help out at the Academy."

"If there's room. You kill me, kid. You just don't assume anything, do you?" Hartfield pushed up from his chair with a wince, then closed the door to the outer office. He came back and sat down in the chair next to Michael. He lowered his voice. "Captain Peterson already knows everything I'm about to tell you, but I don't want anyone else wandering by to hear."

Michael nodded.

"You may have noticed I've dropped a few pounds here lately. Not that I couldn't have used that, but it's not for a very good reason." He drew a deep breath and leaned forward slightly. "I've got cancer, Michael."

Michael leaned back away from Hartfield, absorbing the blow.

"Cancer. Okay, cancer. They've got treatments for that these days, don't they?"

"They do, if you've got the right kind, and if they catch it early enough. I missed on both of those. It's bone cancer, and it's in my spine. I'm dying, and the day's not far off."

"But ..."

"I know it's a lot to absorb. I hate dropping all this on you..."

"I get it. Not a lot of time."

"My problem is, what do I do with the Academy?"

Of course. Curt was going to take over when you retired in ten or fifteen years. But now, Curt's dead, and you will be before too long. So, who could take over? Peterson, maybe? One of the other instructors? They wouldn't just shut the whole thing down, would they?

"I don't have a lot of options. I talked to Peterson about taking over, but he's too old, and he's looking forward to a retirement of his own. He's dreaming of fly-fishing at his cabin in Montana. I sure don't blame him for that. He's kept this place running for years. I can sell it to an outfit that runs an Academy down in New Mexico. Or, I can give it to you."

Michael's head snapped around. "What? Me?"

Hartfield raised a hand, stopping any further objections. "I know, it's crazy, isn't it? You're only eighteen, you just graduated yourself. But, we both know you're wise beyond your years, and I've asked Peterson if he would be willing to delay his own retirement for at least a few more years to let you get your legs under you. Plus, you know Max, and he loves you. It's a package deal—the Academy and Max go together."

Of course. Max. He's going to lose everything, especially if the Academy gets sold to someone out of state. They won't know how to take care of him. They won't recognize all the things he can do, if someone just gives him a chance.

"You know how I feel about Max, too." Michael couldn't bring himself to say, "I love Max." He'd never told anyone he loved them. "But I need to think about this, sir. You understand?"

"Of course I do. If you just jumped at this, I'd be worried about you. But ..."

"Right. I understand. Can I borrow one of the Jeeps again? I want to go for a drive and think about things."

"Get the keys from Captain Peterson. Take a few days. Drive the coast. Peterson will give you some money from petty cash. Let me know what you want to do when you get back."

Chapter Fifty-Five

Michael left the top on the Jeep but rolled down the windows to let the warm summer air rush in. He drove without a plan, without a goal. A small part of his mind kept an eye on traffic, but most of his thoughts were on the future—both immediate and long-term.

I'm at home at the Academy, but is this what I want for the rest of my life? If I accept, I'm tied down. But what happens to Max and the Academy if I don't? Could I just take Max with me wherever I go? Maybe, maybe not. What about the others? Peterson wants to retire soon, but how about the rest of the staff and all the instructors? What about the classes that are coming along behind me?

Michael turned in to a gas station, handed the attendant a five-dollar bill and said, "Fill 'er up."

The pump jockey said, "Yes, sir." A few minutes later, he returned and dropped a few coins into Michael's hand.

Michael looked around to see where he was. He had just been driving for hours, not paying attention to where he was going, but his internal homing device had brought him to what was once home—Middle Falls.

Michael chuckled and shook his head. *Now what? I still have no idea what I want to do. No answers. Turn around and drive home?*

"Home," he mumbled to himself. "That's where home is, now."

One more piece of business here, first.

He drove to the house he grew up in, which still looked the same as it ever did—the grass was green and neatly edged and mowed, the sidewalks swept, and there were flowers blooming in the beds. Michael turned in the driveway and experienced an odd feeling of déjà vu. As if in a dream, Michael walked up to the front door and knocked. He waited a few long moments, then rang the doorbell and heard it bong deep inside the house.

The door opened wide. A woman wearing a maid's uniform said, "Yes?"

"Is Clayton home?"

"Yes ..."

"I'd like to speak to him, please."

"Can I tell him who is here to see him?"

"I'm Michael. Michael Hollister."

No recognition showed on the woman's face.

"His son."

"Oh! Oh, my! Why, yes, of course. Michael."

"It's fine. I would guess he doesn't speak of me often, or kindly. I'd like to speak to him, though."

"Of course, come in, come in. Would you mind waiting here?"

"That's fine," Michael said, but as soon as she left, he wandered through the downstairs. It was immaculately clean, and most of the furnishings were the same as the last time he had seen them, but it felt different in the house. It had never been warm, or cozy, but now it felt hollow and cold, as if whatever life had once been there had been sucked away.

He wandered through the kitchen, lightly touching the fine, bone-handled knife he had once used to kill his father, again and again. He went to the dining room window, which looked out over the backyard. At the rear of the yard, he saw the stump of the tree that had held his tree house in the long-ago. He looked to the left. The low, white fence that had marked the property line between the Hollisters and James Cranfield had been replaced with a tall cedar fence. The gate was gone.

Michael smiled to himself. *Like closing the barn door after the horse has gotten out, isn't it, Father?*

"What do you want, Michael? What trouble have you gotten yourself into now?"

Michael, lost in his thoughts, jumped a bit, then turned to see his father. He had aged terribly over the past ten years. It wasn't just that his hair had gone gray, or that he had gained weight; he looked like a corn husk left in the field to dry.

I'm taller than him, now. I should have known, but it still feels odd.

Michael held his gaze but didn't speak.

Clayton glanced away.

Is he afraid of me now? How ironic.

"If it's money you're looking for, go talk to your mother. I've sent her enough money over the years to take care of everything."

"I don't want anything from you, Father. I didn't know it until just now, but I came here to forgive you."

"Forgive me? For what? Putting a roof over your head? Feeding you? Clothing you? Come on, Michael, you're nearly grown. Time to start acting like a grownup. Get over yourself. The world doesn't revolve around you."

Michael drew in a deep breath, held it, then let it blow out between pursed lips. He nodded to himself.

"You know, you're not the only person something happened to. It happens to a lot of us. But we grow up, we forget it, and we get on with life. That's what I advise you to do, Michael." The words rang bitter and resentful. "Kids today think everything's about them."

Of course. That makes sense. Sorry, Father, the cycle ends here.

"I want to thank you for sending me to Hartfield Academy. I know you did it because you thought I would hate it, and that I would be bullied, or worse, but it's changed everything for me. I've learned about the importance of unselfishly giving yourself, without expecting anything in return. About brotherhood, and hard work. I owe you for that, so thank you."

Clayton snorted. "Big ideas and pretty words don't do much in the real world. Good luck to you with your honor and brotherhood, now that you're out there."

"A friend told me that before you can forgive someone, you have to forgive yourself. I don't know if you're capable of that, but it's what I've been working on. And now, I feel like I can forgive you."

Clayton Hollister took two fast steps and raised his hand, rage blotching his complexion. "To hell with you, you little shit."

Michael didn't move, but Clayton lowered his hand.

"I don't need your forgiveness. All I ever did was take care of you." His breath was coming in ragged gasps.

Michael nodded, then walked past Clayton. As he did, he laid one hand on his shoulder. "Goodbye, Father. I won't need to come back."

Michael walked out the front door.

Inside, Clayton Hollister watched his son's retreating back. He went into his office and sat in the deep quiet. After a minute ticked by, he shook his head vehemently. "Damned, stupid kids."

Outside, Michael climbed into the Jeep and drove off into the sunshine.

Chapter Fifty-Six

Two months later, Curtis M. Hartfield III lay in his bed, covers pulled up tight. The doctors at Crescent City Hospital had insisted he be hospitalized so they could manage his pain. The Commander told them to go to hell.

He was at home, in his quarters at the Academy. Michael sat at his bedside.

"I think you could still bounce a quarter off that bed, even with you in it," Michael commented.

"Max," Hartfield said. The rich baritone was gone, replaced by an old man's rasp. "He wraps me up like a cocoon."

"He wants to do whatever he can to take care of you."

"I know he does. I hate to leave him. I'm so glad we found you, Michael. I don't know what would happen to him if not for you."

"You don't need to worry about that for one minute." Michael paused. "I love him, you know."

"Of course you do. I knew that the day you got into that fight in town."

Michael returned to the book he had been reading aloud, *The Face of Battle,* by John Keegan. He was reading a section about the Battle of Agincourt, and how the British longbows changed military strategy, when Hartfield interrupted him.

"Sorry, my mind wandered. Can you read that last passage again?"

Michael turned back one page and read to the same spot.

"Did you get it that time?" he asked.

Hartfield's eyes were staring blindly at the ceiling.

"Oh." Michael wiped his hand across his mouth, then his eyes.

He touched Hartfield's wrist, then his throat, searching for the thread of a pulse. There was none.

Chapter Fifty-Seven

Carrie feathered her pyxis to a stop. In the frozen picture, Michael sat with his forehead pressed against the blankets of a bed. Beside him was what had once been the man she knew was his friend and father figure. The edge of the picture glowed white with grief.

She had seen many dead bodies as she watched over her charges. The bodies themselves were not a cause of any emotion for her. She could watch the moment the spark of life left the earthly body that had contained it and went on. She knew that life itself was invulnerable.

Still, the impact of someone's departure on one of her people was difficult for her to see.

Detach was her mantra, but detachment had proved elusive for her. All around her, other Watchers did their jobs, unemotionally spinning, twisting, and maneuvering their pyxis to gather the most emotion.

Michael. I hate this pain for you.

She allowed the picture to start moving forward. Another man, whom she knew to be called Max, came into the room. He stopped, shook his head, his hand over his mouth. He lay down on the bed with the body and held it for a long time. Michael stood beside him and hugged him.

Chapter Fifty-Eight
1977

The Earth made another revolution around the sun.

In September 1976, Mao Zedong, chairman of the Communist Party of China, died of a heart attack. In January 1977, Gary Gilmore was put to death by firing squad in Utah—the first execution since the death penalty had been reinstated by the Supreme Court. President Jimmy Carter gave a blanket pardon to Vietnam War draft evaders. In August, David Berkowitz was arrested for the Son of Sam murders.

Michael Hollister, the first non-Hartfield to ever run Hartfield Academy, marked an odd anniversary.

MICHAEL TURNED THE desk calendar to August 22 with a shock.

Today's the day, then. I don't think they make a Hallmark card for "You finally reached the point in time when you killed yourself in your last life," so I won't expect a big celebration. Maybe I'll have two servings of mashed potatoes to go with Iggy's meatloaf tonight.

His first year running the academy had gone smoother than he had expected. There were a few bumps along the way, as he was now overseeing cadets that had been just a year or two behind him. He didn't have the gravitas of Commander Hartfield, but as young Commander Hollister, he quickly showed an affinity for strategy, not just in war games, but in human interaction. The cadets had learned that it was no easier to put something over on Michael than it had been the old Commander.

Curtis Hartfield III had been buried right next to his son in mid-November the previous year. Max had managed to get through playing Taps one more time. When the last note faded, he turned to Michael and said, "I don't want to play that song anymore."

Michael had nodded softly, put an arm around Max, and said, "You don't have to."

Even though he wasn't the Academy bugler any more, Max was invaluable. It turned out that no one could give a tour of the grounds like he could. Among the many attributes of the Hartfield Academy, he never failed to point out that the library was the best military strategy and reference library outside of Washington DC. He charmed every family that came through.

Michael had initially been hesitant to move into the Commander's quarters after Hartfield had died, but he did so at Max's request. They now lived there like the two young bachelors they were. As Michael had suspected, there was indeed a television tucked away in the quarters, and they never missed Max's favorite shows: *Happy Days* and *Little House on the Prairie*.

Captain Peterson had been serious about being ready to retire. Michael asked him to stay for two more years, then begged Will Summers to forgo whatever plans he had and to help him run the Academy. It didn't take much arm-twisting, and Will became Peterson's shadow. Between Michael and Will, the Academy would be in good hands going forward.

And now, Michael was here—August 22, the same day he had hanged himself in his cell in the Oregon State Penitentiary.

A long time ago, Dominick asked me if I believe in ghosts. I think that the me who hanged himself was the ghost, not this me. I don't even know who that person was. I only know I never want to feel that way again.

He closed his eyes.

Thank you for second chances.

He opened his eyes, focused on the folder that lay open on the desk in front of him, and went back to work.

Postscript One

Carrie watched Michael as he sat at his desk, working. The frame surrounding the picture was a quiet gray. *His days are so often quiet, now, and for him, that's a good thing. Maybe it doesn't help me feed the Machine, but what are they going to do? They can't kill me; I have eternal life.*

She made an adjustment to her pyxis and Dominick Davidner appeared, driving a red convertible down a country dirt road. The top of the car was down, the music from the radio was up, and he had one arm slung over the door. He was singing along to the music, loudly and off-key. The frame around him was white.

He's always happiest when he's on the move.

She flipped through the rest of her charges, one at a time. Where she could, she made small adjustments to help each of them. To the universe, all emotion might be the same. Carrie had never mastered the art of detachment, though, and she did what she could to bring happiness into their lives. That translated into contentment in her own life, which also fed the Machine.

She blew a puff of breath straight up to shoo her bangs out of her eyes and focused on a young woman named Emily, who was lying on her bed, reading a book and daydreaming. Carrie switched back and forth between Dominick and Emily, Emily and Dominick. She spun the pyxis ahead rapidly, then feathered it to a stop.

"Just as I thought," she said to herself. "I knew they belonged together. Oh. There's tragedy ahead." She peered into the instrument, looking for a way to help.

Chapter One
The Death and Life of Dominick Davidner
Dimension AG54298-M25735
1999

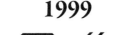

"**H**ey, old girl," Dominick said, laying his hand on Emily's shoulder. "You're going to be late for class if you keep snoozing."

Without opening her eyes, Emily mumbled, "I'm the teacher. I can't be late, cuz they can't start without me." She rolled toward him, a smile parting her lips. She opened one eye. "And what the heck is this 'old girl' stuff? I am still but a child, taken advantage of by an older, lecherous predator."

"Six months. I am six months older than you. That is not exactly robbing the cradle." He brushed her blond hair away from her eyes and kissed her. "Happy anniversary, Mrs. Davidner."

"Oh, please. You know I'm diabetic and can't handle this much sugar in the morning." She groaned as she rolled out of bed and slipped her feet into her slippers. "Maybe you were right the first time. I am an old girl."

An hour later, Dominick kissed her goodbye, standing in the driveway. "Tonight. Dining. Dancing. Maybe even some of that hootchie kootchie I hear the kids talk about."

"Promises, promises," Emily said, then they got into their cars—her Mazda was four years newer than his Subaru, and neither was new—and headed in opposite directions.

LATER THAT AFTERNOON, Dominick sat in the teachers' lounge at Middle Falls High School. "You don't want to handle this last period for me, do you Zack?"

Zack Weaver, the PE teacher and track coach, was in his early forties, but looked younger. He laughed and put his feet up on the table, his hands behind his head. "Me? I'm gonna spend sixth period in my office, getting ready to go home. You are suffering from the weariness of being a real teacher." He winked at Dominick. "This is what you get for being an English teacher instead of a track coach. You've got to actually teach the little buggers."

"Ah, I love 'em, I admit it." He looked sharply at Zack. "Even your twins, who might be just a little too smart for their own good."

Zack shrugged. "Any smarts they got came from Jennifer, not me."

"But," Dominick continued, as though Zack hadn't interrupted, "I want to get out of here early enough that Emily and I might have a shot at beating the traffic in Portland."

"Driving all the way to the big city, huh? Nice."

"Ten years. Ten years she's put up with me. She deserves more than one nice night out in the city, but on two teacher's salaries, that's all she's getting."

Dominick glanced at the clock in the teacher's lounge.

2:03. I better hustle.

"Gotta run," he said over his shoulder to Zack.

He slipped through the door and quick-stepped down the hall to his classroom. He closed the door behind him just as the bell rang.

He smiled at the small class. There were only six students in sixth period AP English. There weren't many kids interested in taking the toughest advanced English class.

"So. Let's continue our discussion of *Lord of the Flies*. Now, where were we?" He flipped his own copy open to the bookmark. "Ah. Right.

We were talking about how both Ralph and Simon are perceived as 'good' characters, but—"

CRACK! CRACK! CRACK!

Three sharp reports from down the hall.

Dominick stopped, held his hand up, and listened.

There were two more reports. Louder. Closer.

Gunshots?

School shootings in Jonesboro, Arkansas; Springfield, Oregon; and Columbine High School had put safety issues at the front of many teachers' minds, but there was no security in place at Middle Falls High, and no locks on the classroom doors yet.

Dominick ran to the light switch and turned the overheads off.

We went over this at the safety meeting. Pull the shades. Turn the lights off. Keep the students in the room.

He turned to the class. Adrenaline rushed through him, but he kept his voice calm.

"Not sure what's happening, but let's take proper precautions. Doug, pull the shades down. Let's make it as dark as possible in here. Everyone else, let's get you into the closet."

He ran to the locked closet at the back and fumbled for his keys. His hands were sweaty and the adrenaline made his hands shake. He got the closet open and hustled the five girls inside. He saw that Doug was pulling the last shade down.

"Hustle up, Doug. Let's see if we can get all of us in the closet."

The classroom door burst open.

Gerald Fleischer, a boy Dominick had taught in an English class the year before, strode in. He had two pistols in his hand, which he held horizontal to the ground, like tough guys do in movies.

Dominick glanced to his right. Doug had frozen in place. The closet door was still open.

Michelle Landry made a small "Eek!" of terror, but reached out and slammed the door shut.

The color ran out of Doug's face. Nowhere to run to, nowhere to hide.

Dominick willed his legs to take one tentative step toward Gerald Fleischer.

Gerald swung both guns to bear on Dominick.

"Oh, hey, Mr. D.," Gerald giggled. "Sorry to fuck with your class schedule. You were a good teacher. I'm not gonna kill you. But," he waggled the gun in his left hand at Doug, "this guy's gotta go."

Without a thought, Dominick launched himself at Gerald.

Time slowed.

Dominick had run track in high school, both the 440 and the 880. That had been more than twenty years ago.

As Dominick dived toward Gerald, arms outstretched, the shooter turned, eyes wide with surprise. He pulled two automatic triggers simultaneously, firing a dozen shots from each gun in just over a second. The bullets from the gun in his left hand ripped through the blinds, shattering the windows. The bullets from the right tracked a pattern from just over Dominick's right shoulder down across his torso.

Dominick jerked backwards, a crimson spray from half a dozen holes arcing across the room.

"Goddamn it, Mr. D! I told you I didn't want to fuck with you!"

Dominick lay face-down on the cool linoleum. A pool of blood spread toward his eye, but he couldn't move.

As consciousness faded, his last words were, "I'm so sorry, Em ..."

Coming Soon:

The Death and Life of Dominick Davidner[1]

Preorder Available Now

---

1. http://amzn.to/2yTgHnk

Author's Note

I want to make a confession. There were times I wished I had never chosen to write this book. And, an update: Now that it's completed, I am so glad I did.

This story began, as so many of mine do, as I was walking my Chocolate Labs, Sadie and Hershey. Dawn and I were living in the bucolic town of Orting, Washington, at the time. In front of our house was a small, man-made lake. It was perfect for late night jaunts with the pups. One night, just as I was finishing the first book in this series—*The Unusual Second Life of Thomas Weaver*[1] —I was walking the dogs around the lake and a phrase popped into my head: *The redemption of Michael Hollister.*

I actually laughed out loud at the idea my subconscious was putting forward. It was ridiculous. I had just spent seventy-thousand odd words creating Michael Hollister as a horrible human being. The last thing I wanted to do was spend more time with him. I knew how I was going to deal with him in that book, and I wasn't unhappy to put him in my rear view mirror.

But then, there's the issue of ignoring your muse. The idea wouldn't leave me alone. When I woke up in the morning, the first thing that popped into my head was those five words: the redemption of Michael Hollister.

So, I cast caution to the wind, and on a whim, I put a brief teaser at the end of *Thomas Weaver*, and then the fateful words: "Coming Soon: The Redemption of Michael Hollister."

---

1. *https://www.amazon.com/Unusual-Second-Life-Thomas-Weaver-ebook/dp/B01J8FBONO*

I was committed. At that point, I had to write it. The problem was, I had no idea how to even begin to redeem Michael. I didn't just dislike him, I hated him. He had killed my favorite character—Carrie Copeland—from that first book. Even worse, I didn't know how to redeem him believably. I couldn't see a path to transitioning from an animal-torturing, murderer to a decent human being.

So, I didn't start on it immediately. Instead, I took my bride, threw a few suitcases in our car and drove all the way around the United States. *That* book, I knew how to write, and I did: *A Lap Around America.*[2] Happily, when that book came out, it sold very well.

That was just the excuse I needed to put off writing about Michael Hollister. I took another nice long drive—this time across The Alaska Highway—and wrote a book about it as well, called *A Lap Around Alaska.*[3]

And then, I was out of excuses, and I still had no idea how to help Michael find redemption. I did the only thing I knew to do. I sat down and just began to write.

Somehow, my subconscious, which had been whispering that title to me for a year at that point, came to my rescue, and Michael's story unfolded, one small piece at a time. When I started the book, I still didn't have any idea where it was going to go, or what Michael's redemption might look like.

Since I'm assuming you've just read that book, you know now that all my dithering was for nothing. I got there. You know what? In the end, I think Michael is my favorite character I've ever written. I'm sure there are lessons in here for me, and eventually, I will figure out what they are.

Now, to the important business of thanking all of the people who helped me bring this book to fruition.

2.   https://www.amazon.com/Lap-Around-America-ebook/dp/B06XY9GSWC

3.   https://www.amazon.com/Lap-Around-Alaska-AlCan-Adventure-ebook/dp/B0744CVWT4

First, is my beautiful bride, Dawn Adele. Many writers thank their spouses, but often, it's just because said spouses left them alone long enough to get the book done. Dawn did so much more than that for me on this book. Every time I was stuck, she and I would talk the situation over, and she would have an excellent idea. For instance, that crisis at the end of the second act, where it looks like Michael is going to have to stay away from Hartfield Academy? All Dawn. She saved my bacon at many turns, and many blind alleys in this book. It's as she often says herself, "It's like I'm practically writing the whole book for you." She's funny that way.

This is the third book I've worked on with my talented editor, Doreen Martens. People think of an editor as someone who corrects grammar, but Doreen does so much for me. For instance, at one point in the manuscript, I had Michael waking up in 1968, instead of 1966. So, when Michael turned the television on in the tree house, I had him seeing an Archies cartoon. Doreen is thorough enough to notice that Michael couldn't have been watching that show in 1966 and saved me from embarrassing myself. She also tirelessly corrects my grammar, too. Especially that whole lay/laid/lying thing, which I can never keep straight. I truly enjoy working with Doreen, and I love that she makes me look like a better writer than I actually am.

The cover for the book was designed by Maria Navillo Saravio from BeauteBook. She also designed the cover for *Thomas Weaver,* and so she is responsible for much of the branding of this series, which I happen to love. She is also infinitely patient with me as I suggest minor tweaks and changes that no one but me would ever notice.

My proofreader on this book, my *last set of eyes,* if you will, was Debra Galvan, who has been with me so long, she is now a certified part of my publishing family. When I give her a book to look over, I think it is perfect. When she gives it back to me, it is always closer to that elusive goal.

I dedicated this book to my writing friend Terry Schott, who serves as the first set of eyes on everything I write. When I doubted I would ever finish this book, he was telling me it was good, and worthwhile. I owe him so much for his support.

I also had a wonderful team of beta readers, including Jeff Hunter, John Draper, Dianne Raymond, Terry Vickers, Laura Heilman, and, I know others, who I am forgetting. I apologize. I always intend to keep a better list, and then forget. Mea culpa.

I almost forgot. Would you like to get a free ebook from me? I am happy to send you one if you sign up for my *New Release Newsletter* here: http://bit.ly/1cU1iS0. I only send emails out when I have a new book coming out, so you'll hear from me four or five times a year. Of course, you can drop off the list at any time. Just for joining, though, I'll send you a free copy of my novel, *Rock 'n Roll Heaven*[4], about a small time rocker who dies and goes to the title place and meets his idols, including Buddy Holly, Elvis Presley, Janis Joplin, Roy Orbison, and more. It's a fun story, and I would love to send it to you.

Up next, is *The Death and Life of Dominick Davidner*[5]. I am looking forward to getting that out to you, as well. If you liked this story, please click over to the next page, and I'll tell you a bit about a few of my other books.

If you'd really like to help me, please go here[6] and leave an honest review. It doesn't matter how long, or what the star ranking is, every review helps.

More than anything, I want to thank you for being a reader. You are what lets me live my dream of being a writer.

Shawn Inmon

Seaview, Washington

---

4.   *https://www.amazon.com/Rock-Roll-Heaven-Shawn-Inmon-ebook/dp/B00J9T1GQA*

5.   *http://amzn.to/2yTgHnk*

6.   https://www.amazon.com/Redemption-Michael-Hollister-Middle-Travel-ebook/dp/B075RPH7HV

October, 2017

Feels Like the First Time[7] – Shawn's first book, about falling in love with the girl next door in the 1970's, losing her for 30 years, and miraculously finding her again. It is filled with nostalgia for a bygone era of high school dances, first love, and making out in the backseat of a Chevy Vega.

Both Sides Now[8] – It's the same story as *Feels Like the First Time*, but told from Dawn's perspective. It will surprise no one that first love and loss feels very different to a young girl than it did for a young boy.

Rock 'n Roll Heaven[9] – Small-time guitarist Jimmy "Guitar" Velvet dies and ends up in Rock 'n Roll Heaven, where he meets Elvis Presley, Buddy Holly, Jim Morrison, and many other icons. To his great surprise, he learns that heaven might need him more than he needs it.

Second Chance Love[10] – Steve and Elizabeth were best friends in high school and college, but were separated by a family tragedy before either could confess that they were in love with the other. A chance meeting on a Christmas tree lot twenty years later gives them a second chance.

Life is Short[11] – A collection of all of Shawn's short writings. Thirteen stories, ranging from short memoirs about summers in Alaska, to the satire of obsessed fans.

A Lap Around America[12] – Shawn and Dawn quit good jobs and set out to see America. They saved you a spot in the car, so come along and visit national parks, tourist traps, and more than 13,000 miles of the back roads of America, all without leaving your easy chair.

---

7.   https://www.amazon.com/Feels-Like-First-Time-Story-ebook/dp/B00961VIIM

8.   https://www.amazon.com/Both-Sides-Now-True-Story-ebook/dp/B00DV5GQ54

9.   https://www.amazon.com/Rock-Roll-Heaven-Shawn-Inmon-ebook/dp/B00J9T1GQA

10.   https://www.amazon.com/Second-Chance-Love-Shawn-Inmon-ebook/dp/B00T6MU7AQ

11.   https://www.amazon.com/Life-Short-Collected-Fiction-Shawn-ebook/dp/B01MRCXNS3

12.   https://www.amazon.com/Lap-Around-America-ebook/dp/B06XY9GSWC

A Lap Around Alaska[13] – Have you ever wanted to drive the Alaska Highway across Canada, then make a lap around central Alaska? Here's your chance! Includes 100 photographs!

The Unusual Second Life of Thomas Weaver[14] – Book one of the Middle Falls Time Travel Series. Thomas Weaver led a wasted life, but divine intervention gives him a chance to do it all over again. What would you do, if you could do it all again?

The Death and Life of Dominick Davidner[15] – Book Three of the Middle Falls Time Travel Series. Dominick Davidner gambles with his life and loses. When he opens his eyes again, he is in his eight year old body, but the pain of losing Emily, the love of his life, is strong. What can an eight year old boy in love do when his future wife is a thousand miles away, and has no idea who he is?

13.   *https://www.amazon.com/Lap-Around-Alaska-AlCan-Adventure-ebook/dp/*
        B0744CVWT4/ref=sr_1_4?s=digital-text&ie=UTF8&qid=1506966654&sr=1-4&key-
        words=shawn+inmon+kindle+books

14.   *https://www.amazon.com/Unusual-Second-Life-Thomas-Weaver-ebook/dp/B01J8FBONO*

15.   *http://amzn.to/2yTgHnk*